You're a mean one, Mr. Chef

LAUREN W. ROACH

Sunflower ROSE
PUBLISHING

Cover Design by Jared Roach at DRMR Creative

Editing by: Tylee Hardman at Markd by Tylee

ISBN: 979-8-9894618-3-7

To those who believe in the magic of Christmas

Chapter One
Audrey

"Okay, how bad is it?" I asked, peeking through my fingers at my best friend Deja as she scrolled through my business Instagram. We sat in my restaurant in the back office before the opening shift began. My staff hustled to prep food and get everything ready for a smooth opening. Deja kept her expression unreadable while she scrolled, which made anxiety simmer low in my stomach. Social media is a mystery to me. I'd much rather stay private, but reels were getting more popular, and I needed to boost my business.

"It's not terrible, per se," she said slowly, chewing on her bottom lip. "But it's not great, either."

I had finally saved up enough money to bring her on as my branding and marketing manager as a last-ditch effort to drum up more business for Audrey's Kitchen. Deja offered free work, but I refused. I'd made her promise to hold a slot for me on her books so we could get started whenever I conjured up the extra funds. Audrey's Kitchen is doing okay financially, but only just barely. Unexpected expenses could leave us underwater.

"You need a stronger social media presence, Audrey. I know you hate socials, but there's no way around it at this point." Deja continued. She took a small sip of the peppermint hot chocolate I had made for her and groaned. "We have to make sure you stay afloat so I can keep getting treats like this."

"What do you suggest I do? I'm at your mercy. Help me, oh wise one." I clasped my hands together and poked out my lips in the silliest puppy dog face I could manage. Deja rolled her eyes; a smirk pulling at the corners of her mouth.

"First, you need more reviews and I added you to a few food related Facebook groups I want you to make a point to be active in." She clicked on her iPad to take notes. "We might even need to film you making a few recipes. The holiday season has really kicked off. Do you have any Christmas treats you could make?" "I have a few ideas, but I don't know if I want to film them. Do I have to wear makeup?" The idea already sounded like it was going to take extra time and effort that I didn't have. Deja glanced up from her iPad, irritation blooming across her face. "Audrey, baby, have you seen yourself lately? You could show up wearing a plastic bag and face paint and would still make hoes mad."

"Shut up, Deja. I'm just saying! That sounds like a lot to do. I just want to cook." I whined, running a hand over my face. "It's not as bad as you make it sound." She stood, taking the empty cup to the kitchen and grabbing her things. "I have to get back to my office. Consider what I said. There's nothing wrong with putting your name out there. It's the only way to survive these days. I'll be back after closing."

As much as I didn't want to admit it, I knew she had a point. I couldn't keep hiding in the shadows if I wanted my restaurant to be considered in the running for the best place to eat. I watched as Deja breezed through the restaurant in her jeans, Jordan 1's, and H.E.R T-shirt. She didn't dress like the typical marketing professional, which helped her stand out amongst the sea of publicists and brand consultants. Her ability to stand out was one thing that made her business so successful, and helped her clients achieve their goals.

With a small sigh, I pulled myself out of the chair and winced. My muscles still ached from leg day at the gym earlier. I had increased weight on the Leg Extension and now my quadriceps were on fire. I didn't mind the pain, though. It let me know I had put in some serious work in the gym. I'd been able to transform my body over the past few years of weightlifting, plus it relieved so much stress. Nothing beats tossing weights after a grueling day.

"You're walking like an old lady." Anika Roman, my little cousin, snickered. I glared over my shoulder at her and continued my ginger steps to the kitchen. I'd be fine after I moved around a little. Sitting still is what caused me to get sore. Anika followed behind me, unafraid to make herself comfortable in my establishment.

"It was leg day." I replied, grabbing my apron off the hook in the kitchen's corner.

She nodded. "I saw this workout on Tik Tok that I've been dying to try." Her long purple box braids swung behind her as she picked up a stack of menus to bring with her to the receptionist stand. "And I saw the cutest outfit to go with it on, SHEIN." I half listened as she gushed about the last movie she had seen on Netflix. I needed to review payroll and my budget again. The numbers were my least favorite part of running a business, but it came with the territory.

I had learned everything I knew from my dad before he died five years ago. He had always had a passion for creating new dishes and making food combinations that no one would have expected. He passed on his love of cooking to me. Many nights during my childhood consisted of us creating dishes and forcing my mom to try them. Some dishes were more edible than others, but mom was always a good sport about it.

When I approached my dad and told him I was going to open a restaurant, he supported me every step of the way. My first meal made in this kitchen was for him. I couldn't officially open for business until he'd given his stamp of approval. On the day of the car accident that took him away from me, I'd called him to tell him I'd gotten my first feature in the local food magazine. He'd been so proud of me and promised to stop by after work so we could celebrate. That was the last time we spoke.

"Oh! Did you see the latest comments on your Facebook post?" Anika asked, showing me her phone. My last post was on the screen. Most comments raved about the shrimp and grits, but one stood out. That single word shattered my mood.
Montrell Davis: ... *Interesting.*

It was a simple enough comment, but it got under my skin all the same. Every word that came out of his mouth rubbed me the wrong way. Montrell has irritated me since we met back in Culinary School. He always felt the need to criticize my recipes, calling them amateur or lazy. When I'd found out he was the one that opened The Hungry Hippo two doors down, I was furious. It felt like a personal attack on my restaurant and made it that much more difficult to bring in the business I needed.

He'd entered my establishment, nose upturned, surveying the place. I wanted to curse him out and tell him to leave, but we were busy, and I didn't want trouble at work. I'd never seen him eat any of the food from my kitchen, but he had the nerve to act as if it disgusted him. I'd chalked it up to him being hateful and assumed he was just raised that way, but his brother dated one of my best friends, Elodie, and was nowhere near as haughty and judgmental as Montrell was.

He and his business partner, Jai, were always competing with what we had going on here. If we were running a sale, they would immediately start running a sale of their own. If we had a theme going on, now they had a theme going on. Every idea I had, they ended up biting off of it somehow. I'd ignored it at first, but the more it happened, the more annoyed I became.
"God, he makes me sick!" I spat, rolling my eyes. Anika's brows furrowed as she pulled the phone back from my line of vision and looked at the picture again.

"Who are you- oh. Montrell? I wasn't talking about him. I meant the rest of the comments." She slid her phone back in her pocket and reached for the menus again.

"Why would he say interesting like that? As if it was a thinly veiled insult. He is such a jerk. I can't stand him."

"I bet you can't." The sarcasm in her tone made me narrow my eyes at her.

"We have a restaurant to open. Go." Just the sight of his smug smile in his profile picture pissed me off and starting the shift in a foul mood guaranteed I wouldn't have the best day. When Anika left the office, hurrying to get the receptionist area presentable before people entered, I took a deep breath and rolled my shoulders back. I wouldn't let him ruin a good day.

"Whew. That was a busy shift." Anika breathed, switching the sign from "open" to "closed" on the door. The rest of the closing staff busied themselves with shutting the building down for the night. I headed back to my office to take a quick peek at the books. It felt like we had more of a crowd today, but I wanted to look at the numbers to be sure.

"Go home, Anika. And tell my auntie I love her when you see her." I called over my shoulder. She nodded and grabbed her things. My little cousin was a life savior when it came to the restaurant. She'd also had a passion for food and wanted to learn as much as she could. She was ready to help wherever needed. I wouldn't be here without her.

By the time I pulled up to my apartment, my entire body was screaming for rest. I couldn't wait to take off my clothes and snuggle under my blankets after a nice, hot shower. I unlocked my front door and stooped to give my Goldendoodle, Chili, a hug. She touched her nose against the side of my face in greeting. I had gotten her three years ago as a present to myself, and she has been my source of comfort ever since.

When the whole world expected me to be the calm and level-headed Audrey, I could come home to Chili and let my guard down in peace. She would never judge me, never question me, just lay her head on my knee while I cried and snuggle next to me when I was ready to go to sleep.

"Hey girl, did you have a good day?" I whispered, rubbing her fur. Chili's tail wagged as she stared up at me with those same big round eyes that had me feeding her pieces of food from my plate. Even though I had vowed not to be the dog mom that would give her pup human food, one look into those brown eyes had me melting into a puddle every time.

Chili trudged along behind me as I put my things down, fixed a quick dinner, and settled into my bed to catch up on new episodes of Station 19. My best friend Monae, being a female firefighter herself, made it one of my favorite shows. It gave me the false sense of understanding her job and feeling like I could be out there with her, running headfirst into danger. She was the only one out of my group of friends that had a dangerous job, and I was in awe of her constantly. Even though it meant that she could not join us for every single Novel-Tea Book Club meeting or take part in every Friend FaceTime, we still held a space for her. Just in case.

I'd just finished an episode when my phone rang. It was Deja. I had figured she would call since she didn't come back to the restaurant like she'd promised. I sighed, not in the mood to hear about something else I was doing wrong or needed to work on.

"Hey Deja."

"What about a cooking competition?" She asked, completely ignoring my greeting.

"Say more words."

"Oh. Right. Okay, so I was brainstorming ideas for ways to bring more people in and get your name out there. The reels are cool, but I found this cooking competition that would actually be great for you." Her words tumbled out quickly, full of excitement and nervous energy.

"A cooking competition? Where?" I paused the television, smirking to myself at the way the characters had frozen on the screen. I put the phone on speaker and sat up. Chili grumbled at the shift in my position but readjusted so her head was resting against my legs.

"It's actually here in town. Isn't that crazy? It's a three round Christmas cooking competition. I'll send you the details. I took the liberty of signing you up already and paying the registration fee because- "

"Deja! Why would you do that? I haven't even agreed to it yet!" I groaned.

"The registration closes today, and I didn't want you to miss out on this opportunity. Don't worry, you can pay me back with the prize money when you win."

My interest piqued. "Prize money, you say?"

"I knew that would change your tune," Deja laughed. "I'll text you the details. You're going to do great! Love you, bye!" She hung up before I responded or to protest.

As if she could understand what was being said, Chili let out a woof in agreement and wagged her fluffy tail. I sighed. A cooking competition was not on my bingo card for the year, but if Deja had already signed up, then I felt obligated to go through with it.

My phone buzzed with a text message. Deja had sent the details of the competition in a screenshot. I clicked the picture to make it fill the screen and read over the rules.

SLEIGH THE RECIPE!
RULES OF THE COMPETITION:

1. MAKE SOMETHING ORIGINAL AND DELICIOUS
2. USE ONLY THE INGREDIENTS PROVIDED BY THE KITCHEN
3. FOOD SAFETY AND HYGIENE STANDARDS MUST BE FOLLOWED AT ALL TIMES
4. PAY ATTENTION TO PORTION SIZES AND QUANTITIES IN ORDER TO REDUCE FOOD WASTE

The winner will receive ten thousand dollars to put towards their restaurant and a feature in The Buzzing Business Magazine

The directions seemed simple enough. Three rounds, with three original recipes. We'd be graded on taste, presentation, and time-management - all areas that I excelled in. The more I read over the rules and looked through the list of businesses that were sponsoring the competition, the more my excitement bubbled inside of me.

"What do you think, Chili girl? Should I do it?" I asked, glancing up at my dog. She tilted her head to one side and stared at me. Her pink tongue hung to the side. "It would be a great opportunity. Who knows? Maybe this is exactly what I need."

Chapter Two
Montrell

"Any holiday plans this year?" Jai, my business partner and best friend, asked me as we got the restaurant ready to open for the day. The Hungry Hippo was our baby. Jai was the brains behind the operation, and I was the manpower. I'd wanted a place to call my own after not having much luck working as head chef in a few restaurants in town. My ideas always seemed to clash with the owner of the business at some point and I tired of making myself small to not offend others. I was feeling stressed and uncertain about my position in the kitchen when Jai called me with the answers to all of my problems.

When Jai approached me about opening the business, I seized the chance. I poured all of my resources and extra cash into this venture and so far; it has proven to be a smart choice. We aren't booming just yet, but we are doing well for ourselves as a fledgling business.

Jai had an eye for business. I'd been nervous working so closely with someone from my personal life, but things were smooth. I'd heard so many horror stories about going into business with friends and family that I wanted nothing to ruin my friendship with Jai, but I should have known that wouldn't be the case. We were too solid for that.

"No plans. I'm sure my parents will expect me to show up at their place at some point. Especially since my brother, his girlfriend, and his adopted son will be there." Last year, my brother Mekhi had brought in an emergency foster named Kellan. The entire family had fallen in love with him and when it came time to leave for his permanent placement, Mekhi had applied for the foster to adopt track so Kellan could stay with him.

His generosity was admirable, and Kellan was a sweet kid, but that is not something I could ever envision myself doing. It sometimes left me questioning myself. After fostering us, our parents adopted my brother and me. But that path wasn't one I envisioned for myself. I wanted my own children. Little babies that looked like a combination of me and whoever I committed my life to.

"How is the kid adjusting?" Jai brought in a box of potatoes and stacked it next to the others, while I made sure the prep was finished so we could open on time.

"He's doing well. Smart kid. Mekhi finally has someone else to annoy with his piano lessons." We both laughed. Mekhi had begged me for years to learn piano and as much as I hated to disappoint him, I hated piano lessons even more. Fortunately for my brother's ego, Kellan seemed to love piano lessons. He absorbed everything my brother said, treating it as a scientific fact. The sight was charming, but I'd never say it. Mekhi didn't need any other reasons to make his enormous head swell even larger. I appreciated that it slowed him down and kept him closer to home. Before Elodie and Kellan entered his life, my brother was all over the place, performing as a pianist. He rarely stayed home for so long, but with a family, his traveling slowed. I was happy to have him close by again.

"That's so crazy, how he went from single bachelor to ready-made family in one holiday season." Jai shook his head. He had a point. Last year was a wild year for my brother, but I was thrilled that he finally had the family he had always wanted. Kellan was a great kid, and Elodie was a positive influence on them both. She seemed like a sweet girl. I wish I could say the same for her friend, Audrey Bennett though. She owned the restaurant a few doors down called Audrey's Kitchen and her ridiculous methods in the kitchen were too much for me to get along with.

Our paths originally crossed in culinary school, and her lackadaisical approach to cooking stressed me out. Don't get me wrong, I am as laid back as they come in my personal life, but in the kitchen? Definitely not. Kitchens require strategy. You must follow recipes, otherwise, that is how you make a mess. This is how errors occur, leading to illness. I made that mistake once and I wouldn't let it happen again. In the kitchen, Audrey never felt bound by rules, always cooking however she pleased. It felt lazy and unprofessional. Too much risk taking in the kitchen can be dangerous, and as many times as I tried to tell her that while we were in school, she had no interest in hearing me out. We spent most of our days in the program fussing with each other and judging each other's dishes. It was a shame we couldn't get along, because she has always been painfully and unfairly beautiful. Her deep hickory skin, full lips, and even fuller hips made it hard to stay irritated while in her presence, but I continued to try my hardest. Underneath the beauty was an untapered chaos I couldn't deal with.

"Hey boss?" One of my waitstaff poked his head in.

I glanced up from what I was doing. "Yeah?"

"There's someone here to see you."

I put my stuff down and followed him out to the front area. When I saw who he was talking about, I had to resist the urge to roll my eyes. Her fire engine red wig gave her away without her even having to turn around. Irritation crept up my spine. Shawna, my ex-girlfriend, stood in the middle of my restaurant, her foot tapping restlessly.

"Shawna," I said, my tone clipped and unfriendly. But that didn't seem to stop her from breaking out into a smile and throwing her arms around my neck. I stiffened under her touch. After breaking things off with her, I no longer wanted her anywhere near me.

"Trelly!" She giggled, reaching for me; I hated that nickname. "I've been calling you for a few days now. My parents are wondering if you want to come spend a few days in the Bahamas with them for Christmas this year."

I stared at her, unsure whether to believe her or laugh in her face. We had broken up months ago. It was hard to believe she hadn't told her parents yet, but I shouldn't be too surprised. If she had her way, she would still be my girlfriend. We'd be planning our wedding and moving in together right now, but she ruined that. Absence from her dulled the memory of her initial allure. But, back then I was so far gone over her that seeing her in the middle of sex with that man rocked me to my foundation. I moped around for weeks, unable to pull myself together.

"Nah, I'm good."

"Trell! Come on. Just last year you were talking about wanting to get married to me and starting a- "

"That was before you cheated on me, Shawna." I interrupted. My patience was wearing thin with her and this conversation. Yes, I had wanted to marry Shawna at one point. I saw myself spending the rest of my life with her, but all of that changed when I went to her house to surprise her on a random day. I'd gotten off work early, only to see her having sex with her coworker. The same coworker she'd assured me time and time again wasn't an issue. Our future together seemed impossible after that. It's simple. You don't cheat on someone you're supposed to be in love with.

Contrary to what my brother may believe, I am a one-woman man when in a committed relationship. When I'm not? That makes things more adaptable and less rigid. I may have one or two on the roster that I like to rotate whenever I am not genuinely interested in someone. As soon as I decide I want to put my effort into a specific woman, then the rest of them are nonfactors. When I'd met Shawna, she was supposed to be someone I added to the rotation, but I ended up falling for her. That was my mistake - one that I was unwilling to make again.

"Trell, please, you can't seriously still be hung up on that." She waved a hand dismissively. "That was so long ago."

Over her shoulder, I saw Jai pointing to his watch, signaling it was time to get the place running. I focused on Shawna once again and narrowed my eyes.

"Look, we're about to open up. If you want to order food, you're welcome to stay, but this current conversation is over." I stepped around her and headed back to check on the staff without giving her a chance to respond.

"Everything cool?" Jai asked, when I was within earshot.

I nodded, "Ain't nothin' worth thinkin' about." He studied me for a moment, then shrugged and turned back to what he was doing. The quick jingle in the background told me she had decided against ordering, which was fine with me. Constantly reminding her we were no longer together was getting old.

I glanced out the window in the kitchen and stopped. From my kitchen window, I could see the back of Audrey's Kitchen, where Audrey was prepping for the beginning of her own shift. Her long black tresses, pulled up into a high ponytail, made her cheekbones look sharp enough to cut through steel.

I observed her, allowing myself a split second to get lost in the moment. Even if her choices were less structured than mine, she moved with such confidence in the kitchen. I hadn't seen her in any other environments, but watching her prep and work was a sight to behold. It commanded attention.

"Yo! Earth to Trell!" Jai called. I turned to find him standing in the doorway with his hands cupped around his mouth. "What are you gawking at in here, man? You looked spaced out."

He stepped closer and looked over my shoulder. "Ah. That

figures." I glanced at him just in time to see the smirk spread across his face.

"I wasn't looking at her." I lied.

"Okay." His smirk deepened. "Sure. You ready to work or do you need to drool a little more? I can step out if you need a second."

I flipped him off and turned back to what I had come into the kitchen to grab, ready to start another shift. His laughter followed behind me as I turned and left.

By the end of the day, my muscles were sore from bending over the food and making sure everything was pristine. Traffic was steady most of the day, but we saw a surge around dinnertime. There was no shortage of things to do to keep busy. Jai hopped in with the serving team when one of our servers had to leave mid-shift to go pick up her child. A few times, I had gone out and spoken to some customers, making sure they all knew how grateful we were to have them dine with us.

"Okay, so you up for making a quick buck?" Jai asked, as we headed out to our vehicles for the night.

"Depends on what it is."

"It's a cooking competition. Neiman told me about it. I think he knows a few people that are entering."

I stared at Jai, waiting for him to laugh and tell me he was kidding. When he stared back, completely stone faced, I laughed.

"A cooking competition?" I snorted, "For what?"

"The winner gets ten thousand dollars. You know we've been planning to make some upgrades. This could certainly make a dent in that expense. Plus, the visibility could be great for the restaurant." Jai unlocked his truck and tossed the leftovers he had swiped inside.

"I'm not doing that."

"You don't really have a choice at this point. I already signed you up since registration closes in a few hours. It's a Christmas competition, so they're going to want to get started next week."

"You've got to be kidding." I folded my arms across my chest and stared at my business partner. More often than not, his business acumen was something to be studied. He had a good sense of timing and knew when to seize opportunities. Sometimes, however, he got a stupid idea in his head and expected me to just go along with it. Like right now, with this competition.

"It won't be that bad, man. It's nothing but a win. Even if you don't win, and we know you will, you'll put The Hungry Hippo on the map. Isn't that what you wanted?"

I narrowed my eyes. Whenever Jai used something I said in conversation against me, I knew he felt passionately about whatever point he was arguing. It was something I learned after being friends with him for so many years. I also knew he was stubborn. Once set on something, nothing could sway him.

As the silence stretched between us, I could feel my resolve cracking. A cooking contest was not something I had pictured myself doing anytime soon, especially not a contest involving Christmas. I didn't mind Christmas. My mother's years of decorating and creating traditions prevented me from hating it, but I could only tolerate so much holiday cheer before I protested. After a while, Christmas puns can become a bit excessive.

"Fine." I sighed, "But hear me clearly when I say this: I am not wearing any Santa hats."

Jai barked out a laugh and clapped his hand on my shoulder. "That's a fair exchange." We both fell silent again, taking in the night air. It was a little chilly, but not cold enough to be unpleasant. I preferred the colder air, anyway.

"This is a stupid idea. I hope you know that."

"Your faith in my business decisions is overwhelming." He deadpanned, rolling his eyes. It was my turn to laugh. I trusted him with my life, and he knew it.

"I said I'd do it." I shrugged.

"I'll send you the details when I get home. It's slight work, man. You got this in the bag. No doubt."

By the time I made it home, I was already regretting agreeing to do this competition. The idea of a Christmas competition seemed cheesy and pointless. The money would be nice, but I'd much rather just throw a fundraiser or two at the restaurant and call it a day. My phone buzzed with a text from Jai. He had sent over the information for *Sleigh The Recipe*. I smirked at the name as the link loaded on my phone screen.

The competition, spanning three rounds, offered the winner both prize money and the opportunity to be published in a renowned magazine. Originality, time management, and food safety were all requirements outlined in the rules. The process appeared straightforward, affording more space for originality than I expected. It could be fun. It could also be a nightmare.

Chapter Three
Audrey

"God, y'all have no idea how much I've been looking forward to this," Monae groaned, settling onto my couch. Her long, bone straight hair was tied in a bun at the back of her neck. As she relaxed, she reached forward and snatched the pins out, letting it cascade over her shoulders. "That last shift was brutal. Back-to-back fires."

"How many days do you have off?" I asked, passing her the napkins I'd had left over from the last time I hosted the book club. Novel-Tea was a book club that my friends and I started in college. Back then, we were hanging out a bit more often, but as soon as we branched out into our own career paths, this gave us the chance to come together and reconnect.

"I'm off for two. Then I'll be back at the station for two." Monae replied, rubbing Chili on the head. Brina and Deja had already arrived. We were waiting on Elodie. Ever since she and Mekhi got together last year, being able to pull her away from him and his new foster-turned-adopted son, Kellan had been difficult. I thought it was sweet how she just fell into a ready-made family. It's not something I'd choose for myself, but I love seeing her so happy in that dynamic. Mekhi was a great person, and he treated her so well. I couldn't ask for more for my friend.

"Does it ever get scary?" Brina asked, leaning forward in the recliner she had claimed as hers. "Being a firefighter? Especially a black female firefighter. There aren't many of you."

"Sure. Of course, it does. It's a high adrenaline job sometimes, and the added factor of being the only woman on my team can make it tricky to navigate. But those are my brothers, and I wouldn't trade what I do for anything." Monae plucked a Rolo Pretzel Bite off the platter and popped it into her mouth. It was a new recipe I had decided to try, and from the look of ecstasy on her face, it was clearly a hit.

"God, Audrey, how do you keep coming up with these things?" She groaned, reaching for another one.

"I'm good at what I do." I shrugged. I pretended it didn't impact me, but my girls' opinions on new recipes mattered the most to me. They would tell me if it was satisfactory or required revisions.

"Where is Elodie?"

"Here I am!" As if on cue, she came bustling into my living room carrying four different gift bags. "Sorry I'm late. Had to get your gifts together." She handed each of us a bag before grabbing a pretzel bite and plopping down on the couch next to Monae.

"I didn't think we were doing gifts this year, El." I said. We'd had a conversation about wanting to focus on families this year and not feeling the pressure of having to get each other presents

Elodie shrugged, "WE aren't. But I am."

Before I could protest, Deja clapped her hands excitedly and sprang to her feet. I had a feeling I knew what she was going to say before she opened her mouth.

"Ladies! I've got news - well, we've got news. Audrey will compete in *Sleigh the Recipe!*" I could feel my face flush as everyone turned to look at me.

"What's *Sleigh the Recipe?*" Brina asked. She got up to refill her wine glass.

"It's a Christmas themed cooking competition." I replied. The sudden nervousness overwhelmed me, making me long to vanish beneath the coffee table. "Deja signed me up without telling me."

"Don't do that." Deja made a face at me. "You know it's a dope idea for your brand. It'll boost visibility and put your name out there."

"Is there prize money?" Brina asked.

I nodded, "ten thousand."

"Period!" Monae pointed at me, "Lock in, Audie. You got this. Just make these pretzel bites. I could eat a whole pan of them myself."

"Or you could make those Thanksgiving Wontons you made for Friendsgiving. I've been dreaming about them ever since." Brina sighed.

I looked around at my girls, feeling overwhelmed by the

amount of support they had for me. For the next few minutes, they pelted me with ideas for treats to try and things to do with the prize money as if I had already won the contest. I soaked it all in, missing my dad more than usual. He would have loved something like this. Any excuse to brag to the world about his chef daughter.

"I guess this is as good a time as any." Elodie stood up and reached for the gift bags she had brought in with her. She passed one out to each of us. Mine was in a shimmering green bag. Excess glitter lingered on my fingertips as soon as I touched it.

"Is this the new cookware set with the floral handles that I have been begging for?" I asked, shaking the bag. Elodie grimaced and shook her head. I pulled out the tissue paper and glanced down at the bag to reveal an old, leather-bound journal with a delicate feather pen.

The same journal that had Elodie freaking out last year. Her grandmother had given it to her, claiming that it would write her love story for her. She simply had to let it work its course. Coincidentally, things started heating up with Mekhi after she received the present from her grandma, but that was just a case of convenient timing. I had humored her at the moment, my attention split between that and the future of my restaurant, but I hadn't realized she had taken it this seriously. I was frozen, unsure how to react. Why was she giving me this journal?

"El, why are you giving me this?" I asked, glancing up at my friend. She wore a mischievous grin as she watched me open it.

"What is it?" Monae asked, craning her neck to see. Beside her lay a box that contained a beautiful gold necklace with a

Firefighter Axe pendant on it. I couldn't make them out from where I sat, but I saw it had engravings on it.

"Her lil spooky journal from last year." Brina laughed, shooting me a sympathetic smile.

"It's not spooky, Brina. Look, I can't explain how any of it works. I just know that it told me it was your turn."

"It told you?" I asked, the skepticism clear in my voice. "You want me to believe this book talked to you?"

Elodie rolled her eyes and opened the front of the journal. In blocky letters read: **This Journal Belongs to Audrey Bennett.**

It didn't look like her handwriting; I'd seen her sloppy script plenty of times in her notebooks during college. We'd shared a dorm room, and she'd constantly leave her notebooks lying around, full of haphazard scribbles as she tried to take notes on the lectures. The closer I looked at it, the more I realized it resembled my handwriting. And that was impossible. I hadn't touched this journal until right now. Whoever wrote in it was talented at copying penmanship. I looked up to see Elodie scrutinizing me, watching my face for any sign of what I was thinking.

"I don't know, El. This seems silly."

"I know it does. I shared the same sentiment until I met Mekhi."

"Is that why you rode the dick so soon?" Monae giggled, "Because the journal told you to?"

Elodie gasped and tossed a pillow in her direction, which made

Monae laugh even louder. The exchange inspired Elodie to gush about the newest developments with her and Mekhi. They were still on track to adopt Kellan, and Mekhi had been dropping hints of proposing soon. Elodie had a list of engagement rings that she'd want just in case he reached out to any of us about helping him pick something out. I listened as she talked excitedly, and thought about the last year of our lives.

Elodie and Mekhi's relationship progressed much quicker than I expected, but they seemed to be genuinely happy together. They'd fallen in love last Christmas season and while I had originally thought it was just the magic of the holiday that caught them slipping, they ended up lasting well beyond that. While she continued to talk, I slid out of my seat and put the journal on my nightstand in my room. Despite my doubts about the book's magic, I would still protect it until she asked for it back. It was the least I could do as a friend. I didn't anticipate needing it much otherwise. My focus is entirely on the contest. Romance can wait. I had a lot on my plate until then. When Audrey's Kitchen was booming like I had hoped it would be by now, I could pause long enough to focus on love.

"Call me tomorrow! Love you!" I called after the girls as they all headed towards their cars at the end of the night. We'd spent most of the evening catching up and eating the snacks I had made. We had just finished The Memory Concierge by Lauren Roach. I'd cried throughout most of the story, as did Elodie, Monae and Brina, but Deja had admitted that she didn't enjoy it. No matter how much we tried to convince her it was a good story, she was not having it.

The next book we were supposed to read was one by an author I had never read before, S. A. Cosby. He was a black male author that wrote thrillers, primarily set in Southern towns. It was a vibe that I rarely went for, but Monae had complained that we kept picking 'sappy love stories' and wanted something with a little more grit and suspense. We had debated for a while on which one to start until we finally tried 'All Sinners Bleed'. I had downloaded it on my Kindle and was eager to get started. I planned to at least get a chapter or two read after I finished cleaning the kitchen.

My girls devoured all the snacks, leaving me with just the dishes and countertops to clean. I couldn't stand going to sleep with a dirty kitchen. It would make me toss and turn all night, unable to fully rest until it was completed. Chili waited dutifully by the kitchen doorway as I made sure everything was clean before shutting off the light and making my way to the bedroom.

I felt an exhaustion deep in my bones. There was so much to do. I had to carefully review the contest rules, brainstorm recipes that met the time and ingredient requirements, and choose an outfit that was both comfortable and practical.

Instead of getting a jump start on any of that, I slid into bed with my Kindle and opened the book I had just downloaded. Those problems could wait until tomorrow. Chili hopped up on the bed and took her usual spot laying across my legs. She was like my very own fluffy, weighted blanket. Some days, it really helped to calm my nerves.

I'd just gotten to chapter two in the book and was engrossed in the story when Chili, who had been dozing peacefully, popped awake. Her head tilted to the side in curiosity as she listened to something I couldn't hear with my human ears.

"What is it, girl? What do you hear?" I asked. She pushed herself up into the sitting position, eyes locked on the journal that had been resting on my nightstand. I looked over at it, curious. Chili abruptly barked. I put my hand on her back, hoping to calm her, but it didn't work. Her gaze was fixed on the journal. Out of the corner of my eye, I saw something move.

The journal lay open, its pages fluttering as if caught in a breeze. I stared, opened-mouthed, at the journal that was moving completely on its own. Chili's bark continued to ring out through the house, but I barely noticed it. I focused on the journal, puzzled by its movement. Part of me wanted to call Elodie and cuss her out for giving me something undeniably possessed.

"What is happening right now?" I mumbled to myself. The pages continued to flip backwards and forwards until it settled on the first page. As I watched, terrified and intrigued, words appeared on the page as if something was standing over it, writing. The words quickly filled the page, one after the other, until it was completely covered in writing.

And then it stopped.

The pages stopped moving; the words stopped appearing, and Chili stopped barking as if her life and mine depended on it. Everything went still. Time felt like it had frozen. The only thing that existed in this moment was me, my dog, and this journal. I crept forward, breath hitching in my throat, until I was directly in front of it. The words were written in the same handwriting, one that mirrored my own so closely.

My hands trembled in fear as I reached for it, bringing it closer to my face so I could read the message. I finally understood how Elodie must have felt the first time it happened to her. If it was anything like this, no wonder she had been so scared of it. I held it up and began reading, resisting the urge to throw up in my mouth as I read. This couldn't be right. Chili pawed at my leg, whining softly, but the only thing I could focus on were the words on the pages in front of me. The more I read, the more I wanted to crumble this page up and throw it in the nearest trash can. It felt like a mockery, an insult. Knowing how much I abhor him, knowing how much even the mention of his name sparks a visceral reaction inside of me. And yet...

Dear Diary,

Today, something shifted between Montrell and Audrey. Culinary School's tension persisted, but a fleeting shift occurred. Montrell's glance lingered longer as he observed her through his own kitchen window, and Audrey, for once, didn't dismiss the mention of his name.

It was brief, just a second, but it was there — a crack in the armor they've both so carefully built around themselves.

It's funny, because as much as they clash, there's an energy between them. Energy that others can perceive. It might be

because of past resentment, but you can't shake the feeling that there's something deeper. It's as if the friction has built up enough to spark something else entirely. Maybe the tension is just a symptom of something more profound.

It's doubtful either of them would admit it, not yet at least. They seem too invested in disliking each other. But feelings are tricky like that. You can push them down, ignore them, or even mistake them for something else. Still, we can't shake the feeling that something's beginning to change between Montrell and Audrey. This animosity has just been the surface all along, and beneath it, something else is growing.

Only time and competition will tell if they'll continue to fight — or if they'll find themselves feeling something else entirely.

Chapter Four
Audrey
Six Years Earlier

"Okay, class, your assignment is to work with your partner to create two viable businesses. In the second phase of the project, you'll create a meal and feed it to the final panel of judges. This determines whether you graduate the course. So, I suggest you take it seriously." My instructor folded his burly, tattooed arms in front of him and glared at each of us in mock sternness. It was me and seven other students in a tiny, up close and personal style classroom and kitchen combination. The workstations, each having a small stove and oven, facilitated simultaneous cooking.

I loved being in such an intimate setting. It gave me the chance to know all of my classmates by name and study their cooking styles. Montrell Davis included. He was the only person I wished wasn't in this class with me. His presence sucked up all the air in the room, making it hard for me to catch my breath. I had been avoiding him ever since I'd overheard him flirting with one of my friends during orientation.

To my dismay, everywhere I went, he ended up showing up at some point, usually late and with some superficial wannabe model on his arm. The girls' drooling over him, while he remained indifferent to their attention, was repulsive.

What surprised me, though, was that when we were in the kitchen, that nonchalant attitude he constantly sported was gone; replaced by a rigid and rule-obsessed tyrant. It made it completely impossible to try anything new around him. Strict adherence to rules and procedures was mandatory. That mindset made him bump heads with my relaxed way of operating in the kitchen.

It always confused me how opposite his personality was from the way he moved around the kitchen. Cooking triggered a transformation in Montrell, as if a switch flipped and a wall rose, replacing his usual demeanor. The nonchalant personality was replaced with a dictator who demanded strict order and control.

The point is to learn the rules so that you can break them. How else would you discover anything new? What other way is there to learn how to create dishes that everyone else would enjoy? How else would you make something that no one else had made before? This is how all recipes are created. There was a time when nobody knew how to cook until they continuously experimented to find out what worked. You had to step outside of the box at some point. Otherwise, you would be boring. People don't enjoy boring.

"I'll be picking your groups." My instructor continued, taking slow and deliberate steps in the front of the classroom. I watched

him as he moved, envious of his confidence. I desired that
same confidence, both in cooking and in life beyond food. He
continued to speak, relishing our fascination. He captivated us,
and he was aware of it. A legendary cook and culinary expert,
he was known far and wide. He had been the personal chef for
a long list of celebrities before retiring to teach us here in this
culinary arts class.

"Blackman, you will be paired with Craig. Bennett, you will
be with..." He surveyed the class. I closed my eyes, praying and
hoping against all hope that it wouldn't be Montrell. Anyone else
but him. Please, not him. It felt like an entire year had passed in
the few seconds it took him to pick my partner. I held my breath,
hoping I would get lucky and not have to deal with-

"You'll be with Mr. Davis."

"Ugh!" I grumbled. It should have been obvious. From where
he sat to my left, I could feel Montrell's eyes on me. I kept my
gaze on the front of the classroom. I remained muted while the
rest of the pairs were called out.

"Alright. Work with your partners. Let's review the menus
we've been working on and see what creative ideas you can come
up with. Class dismissed." Everyone stood, grabbing their things
and talking amongst their peers. I gathered my things and turned
to leave the classroom when I bumped into what felt like a brick
wall.

"Oof!" I grunted, stepping backwards. I glanced up and saw
Montrell smiling down at me. My stomach flipped. "What?" I
asked.

"Can we quickly review what we both have?" He asked.

"How do you know I don't have plans?" I countered,
narrowing my eyes at him. He gawked at me and then laughed

like I had said the funniest joke he'd ever heard. Embarrassment made my cheeks flush, and I looked away, unable to stomach his reaction.

"Let's sit over here." He motioned towards a now empty table, completely bypassing my question. His lack of consideration for my plans, whether they were real or not, upset me. Just because I didn't have people falling all over me like he did, didn't mean I was without friends. It didn't mean that I couldn't have plans after class; I had none, but he didn't have to know that.

"Let's make this quick. I've got somewhere to be soon." I ignored the incredulous look he gave me and put my things down on the table he had led us to. Being around him stirred up irritation and annoyance inside of me I couldn't explain. I constantly felt tense, anticipating his next outburst that would inevitably lead to another argument.

"Let's see what you got," He said, pointing to my bag. I hesitated for a second, not wanting to show him what I had been working on. It was special to me, and I didn't want him to ruin it. I finally sighed and pulled out the menu and the budget I had been working on and slid it across the table towards him.

"It's called Audrey's Kitchen" I mumbled. I had been trying to find names that would be cute and cliche, but Audrey's Kitchen fit the best to me. It was me and it was mine. My food, my decor, and my vibes would be what would bring people in and keep them.

"This is an interesting menu." Montrell said, glancing quickly at it, "It's a little all over the place."

I glared at him, irritated that I had spent so much time on this menu only for him to brush it off without so much as a perfunctory glance. "What's wrong with it?"

"You know how we usually calculate food cost. It's beginning inventory value plus all monthly purchases minus ending inventory, divided by total food sales." He rattled off the same information we had gone over in class earlier that day.

"Yes, I'm aware of that." I snapped, rolling my eyes. "I've accounted for all of that in this menu creation."

"What's the theme of this menu? Because I can't tell by looking at it."

"It's a contemporary twist on soul food." The more he scrutinized my work, the less confidence I felt in the final product. I wanted to take it out of his hands and crumbled it into a ball. The self-doubt made me angry. Why did this jerk rattle me so much?

"Interesting." He sniffed, squinting at the items I had listed. "Your food costs would be crazy high with something like this. Hardly seems sustainable at the prices you've listed."

"Well, do you have something better?" My tone was sharp. He raised an eyebrow but pulled a piece of paper out of the three ringed binder that was sitting in front of him. It was a menu for a restaurant called The Hungry Hippo.

I smirked. "This is a dumb name. Why did you pick it?" I searched for ways to hurt his feelings in the same way his comments about my menu had hurt mine. Instead, he stared at me with an unreadable expression before shrugging his broad shoulders and flashing a nonchalant grin.

"I was a fat kid growing up. They used to call me Hungry Hippo in school. So, I figured why not put that stupid nickname to use?"

I immediately felt like a jerk. "Sorry. I don't hate it."

Montrell laughed. It was a rich sound I could feel in my gut.

I squirmed in my seat, my entire body flushing with heat. We were the only two sitting in this part of the classroom. Everyone else had gone home for the day and suddenly I wished there was someone else here with us. Someone to distract me.

"It's fine. I don't expect everyone to love it. But listen, your menu needs work."

Just like that, when I had warmed up to him a little, he had to remind me he was trashing something I'd worked hard on. I folded my arms across my chest and glared at him, not willing to budge.

"My menu is fine."

"If you want us to get an acceptable grade on this assignment, then you'll let me help you."

His arrogance was upsetting. Who died and made him King of the Kitchen? He stared at me, his light eyes full of amusement. I don't know why his comments were ripping through me. I should be able to accept criticism, especially when it came from someone who had no control over my grades or success in the program, but every time he made a comment concerning my dishes or my menu choices, I felt the need to fight.

"Are you always this arrogant?" I asked.

"Are you always this stubborn?" He countered, waving the menu in my face. I snatched it out of his grip and smacked it down on the table. My sudden movements made his eyebrows shoot up, curiosity and something else flashing in his eyes.

"My menu is fine. My ideas, great. Read my lips. Audrey's Kitchen will be successful one day."

"Not with this haphazard menu and your inability to use any kind of structure in the kitchen, you won't."

Ready to escape his presence, I stood. I turned to leave, then

thought against it, choosing instead to get closer to him. I stepped
into his personal space, reveling in the uncomfortable shift in his
expression.

"Audrey's Kitchen will thrive. I will be successful. Watch me."

"Take it back!" I screeched into the phone. It was four in the
morning, and I hadn't been able to sleep ever since this stupid
journal told me that Montrell and I were supposed to be starting
something. "Take it back, right now!"

"Wha-? Take what back?" Elodie groaned. Sleep made her
voice raspy and deeper than usual. I had woken her up before her
alarm, but at this moment I didn't care. It's her fault for giving
me the devil's notepad and setting me up to get spooked when
I already had more than enough to be focusing on. I should
be sleeping myself, but I'm wide awake, pacing the floor like a
madwoman. She was going to take this journal back, and she was
going to take it back today. I wanted it out of my house with the
quickness.

"This possessed piece of garbage you tried to pass off as a
Christmas present!" I hissed. Chili's ears flattened, not used to
hearing me sound so angry.

"Did it start working already?" Elodie sounded much more
alert, interested even. "Wow. That's impressive."

I narrowed my eyes. "You didn't tell me this thing was
possessed. Why would you bring it to my house?"

Elodie giggled, "Breathe, girl. It's not dangerous. Just a little
magic. And you're the one that said we could all use a little
Christmas magic, right?"

"When did I say that?" I asked, confused.

"Last year, when I was in your spot, figuring out how a journal could write on its own."

"Elodie," I sighed, rubbing my forehead, "I was clearly just being supportive. If I had known this thing would be talking nonsense, I would have told you to keep it."

"What did it say?"

"It's pairing me with Montrell Davis!" I spat. "Of all people!"

"Ah. There it is." Elodie replied. I could hear the smile in her voice. She's lucky we weren't in the same room, so I could wipe that smirk right off her face. I heard rustling in the background and then Mekhi's deep voice.

"Is everything okay?" He asked Elodie.

"Tell him that his brother is an ass!" I yelled, while she responded to him. His responding chuckle told me she didn't need to pass along the message. Mekhi was a cool person; I didn't mind him at all. I couldn't understand how someone so arrogant and bigheaded could be his brother.

"He shows his good side occasionally; he's not so bad once you get to know him." Mekhi's voice was muffled, followed by a soft click. When Elodie spoke again, there was a slight echo, telling me she had stepped into the bathroom for a bit more privacy. I felt bad for waking up the both of them, but this journal had me freaking out. Montrell cannot possibly be my match. Obviously, this journal was defective.

"So, be honest, is it the journal that's the problem or who it's telling you your match is?" She asked.

"He's so mean! Did you see that comment he left on my last food post?"

"No. Let me go look." She was muted for a minute as she

pulled up my last Facebook post. I waited patiently for her to scroll through the comments until she found his. "It says 'interesting'. Is this the comment you're talking about?"

"Like, what does that even mean? Interesting? Pfft." I sniffed. "He is just pissy because he can't cook like I can."

"Audrey," she began slowly, I could tell she was choosing her words carefully, "There has always been some weird energy between you two. I know little about your past with him, but I know people can change. People can grow. You both were so young when you met."

"You're supposed to be on my side." I grumbled, sinking back down on my bed. Chili licked my free hand.

"I am on your side, Audie. The side that brings you unimaginable joy. I don't pretend to know exactly what fuels this journal, but I do know that you deserve something beautiful. Maybe this is it."

"I highly doubt it."

"Girl. Goodbye. I'm going back to sleep." I heard the click of the line in my ear before I could respond. I wanted to call Elodie back and continue fussing, but knowing her, she'd already put her phone on Do Not Disturb until it was time for her to wake up for work. She and Mekhi still worked at Astoria Middle School, and they would likely be getting ready for this year's Christmas program. Last year, while working on the musical, they ended up falling in love. I was excited to see what they had in store for us this year.

With a sigh, I slipped into bed, determined to get some kind of sleep before I was due at the restaurant. With Christmas coming up so soon, I needed to get the Christmas menu together. I kept most items the same, with a few seasonal additions that made it fun for the regulars. I'd have to review the food budget to accommodate the extra items.

The earlier I started, the easier and smoother the transition would be for my other staff members. The competition's start meant less time for me at the restaurant, leaving my staff to keep everything running smoothly. Despite my complete faith in my team, leaving the restaurant for an extended period made me uneasy.

Before I knew it, I had fallen asleep. Letting images of winning the competition and making a name for myself and Audrey's Kitchen fuel my dreams.

Chapter Five
Audrey

"Audrey Angelique Bennett! Why has it been so long since I've heard from you? Are you avoiding me?" my mother yelled into the phone. I winced at the anger in her tone, feeling bad for leaving her hanging. With the contest approaching and restaurant preparations, I hadn't returned her calls, despite her reaching out for days. I knew I was on thin ice with her. I was only one or two phone calls away from her demanding to know where I was. It dawned on me that I should have responded or at least returned her call before things escalated. I'd been embarrassed too many times to risk that again.

"I'm sorry, I haven't been avoiding you. I've been busy."

"You've been busy? Too busy for ya mama? I see how it is." She shot back, softening a bit. I smiled at her feisty attitude. Even in her seventies, that fire I had grown up fearing and then later admiring never dimmed. She was my hero. I'd seen her make grown men cry in her day and she would do it with a smile on her face. When she wasn't commanding the courtroom as a judge, she was taking me to all of my cooking classes and listening to me vent while I tried hobby after hobby until something finally stuck.

She had always been one of my loudest supporters, making sure that I knew I could do whatever I put my mind to, but she was never afraid to pull me back down to earth if I needed. When I was getting too big for my britches, as she liked to say, she had no problem reminding me of who I was and who she was. As a teenager, that had been annoying, but I grew to appreciate it as I got older. She never let me forget where I came from, especially in moments where I let my head get too big by accident.

"Never too busy for you, mama. How are you?" I put the phone on speaker while we talked so I could focus on prepping the kitchen for the next few days. "Are you feeling okay? How has your knee been acting lately?"

Ever since my father passed, I had been worried about her living alone, but she had declined every single offer to move in with me or let Chili and me move in with her. She was determined to enjoy life while she still had breath in her body. I admired her determination, but sometimes I wish she would sit down somewhere. Raising your parent is so hard. They never listen. She was the worst of them, always out and about when she should be sitting at home watching television or taking a nap. Mama was a restless soul, always pursuing new experiences and adventures. Especially now that she was alone.

"I'm fine, little girl. How have you been? Something must be new for you to avoid my calls like I'm the police."

"Just keeping the restaurant afloat. Been working with Deja to do a bit more marketing and advertisement." I wiped the counter and pulled out some vegetables to get a head start on chopping them. "She entered me in a cooking competition. The winner gets ten thousand dollars for their restaurant. My food is good. I need to become more well-known, you know?"

"That's great baby. You'll win. I can feel it in my bones, and you know my bones don't lie."

"Yes, I know, Mama."

"Tell me more about this contest. Will you need to travel for it?" I spent the next few minutes filling her in on what I knew about *Sleigh the Recipe*. My excitement for the contest grew with each word I said. As I talked, she would offer a few grunts or 'mhms' encouraging me to keep talking. I shared with her the recipes I was thinking about trying and what I would do with the money if I won. It felt good to talk about it with her. Talking with my mama made everything feel real. She listened without interrupting and before I knew it, I'd had everything chopped and separated. I blinked down at my cutting board, surprised. Didn't realize I had been cutting while I was talking, my body moving on autopilot.

"Your father would be so proud of you." She whispered. "I hope you know that, Audrey." I heard a muted sniffle. My heart clenched in my chest. I missed my dad more than I could explain with words, but I knew anything I felt paled compared to what she felt. They had been married for thirty-seven years and been best friends their entire lives before that. She'd often told me that what scared her the most about him being gone was learning how to live without him around.

She'd admitted to me one night that she'd gotten so used to his presence that everything felt empty and hollow without it. I had always admired their relationship; I'd wanted a love that was deep like theirs. Growing up, I'd rarely seen them argue. Whenever they disagreed about something, they talked it out without disrespecting each other. It was a rare sight. Their love was the one you write stories about and I wanted one of my own.

My mind drifted back to that journal that Elodie had given me. It pushed me toward the one person I despised, claiming my love story stemmed from our mutual aversion. I had trouble believing that someone whose very existence pissed me off was the same person who I would spend my life with. My mind drifted back to the conversation, when I'd realized a moment or two had passed without me saying anything. I could tell that my mama sensed there was something on my mind, but she would not pry.

"My restaurant is struggling. He wouldn't be proud of that."

"Nonsense. The restaurant business is tricky. He understood that, but you are chasing after what you want without letting anyone stop you. That's the thing that would have made him proud. Blinking rapidly, I fought to keep my tears from falling down my face. I missed my dad every single day, even more so now that I was in the restaurant business. I knew he would have been right next to my mom, screaming my name in the stands if he was still here. He was the one who would have made t-shirts and posters. Anything to let the world know that Audrey Bennett was his daughter, and he was unbelievably proud.

"Thanks, mama." She wasn't always emotional, which made the moments she was that much more special.

"Of course." She sniffled. "Now, the real reason I was calling is to ask for your help with dinner this year."

"Seriously?" I whined. Just like that, the mood was ruined. I should have known. She knew I detested holiday cooking because family members always found fault. No matter what you cooked and served them, they were never satisfied. She knew I'd refuse, so she'd always wait until I had no choice but to agree before asking. I ended up falling for it every single time. "Why do I feel like you tricked me into an emotional moment so you could hit me when my defenses were down?"

My mother laughed, all traces of tears and emotion that had been in her voice two seconds ago vanished. "I would never do that. Don't tell me you wouldn't help ya poor mama!"

I rolled my eyes at the phone, even though she couldn't see me. "That was definitely an emotional trap, but luckily for you, I am feeling charitable this year." Her hearty laughter made me smile. I'd endure the holiday drama if it meant we had time to work together in the kitchen.

After we hung up, I finished prepping before Anika and the rest of the staff arrived. I brought in some extra help so I could take some time off and focus on *Sleigh the Recipe*. I wanted to make sure my head was clear the entire time and nothing would distract me from bringing home the prize money.

"Hi, boss lady!" Anika came breezing into the kitchen, purple braids swinging behind her. She tied them up in a lopsided bun on top of her head and smiled at me. "Where do you want me?"

"You're here early." I replied, glancing down at my watch.

"Yeah, I've had to come in a few minutes early to get a parking spot."

"What happened to your usual parking spot?" I asked. Anika averted her gaze. I moved from behind the counter and stood in front of her with my arms folded. "What happened to your usual spot, Anika?" I repeated, narrowing my eyes.

"Customers from The Hungry Hippo keep taking it..." she replied and then winced like I was about to swing. Instead, I breathed in a heavy sigh, tampering down my irritation. "It's not a big deal, though. As long as they don't take spots from the customers, we're fine."

"He'd better not. Or I'm going over there." I snapped, grabbing my apron from the hook on the back of the door. Montrell and his assistant Jai were always ruining my day. Usually I could ignore them, but if it started bleeding into the business, then it would have to be addressed. At least we were okay for now.

"Hi! Welcome to Audrey's Kitchen! Will it just be two of you dining with us today?" I overheard Anika greet a couple as they entered the restaurant. They were a younger looking couple, around college age.

"Yes! Man, I thought you guys would be a little busier in here." The guy remarked, "It took us forever to find a place to park!" Anika whirled around, eyes wide, searching for me. When our eyes locked, she pleaded with me not to do anything.

"So sorry about that," she forced a smile, turning back to the customers, "Let me show you to your table." I watched, fuming, as she led them to one of the empty tables. After handing them the menus and telling them who their server would be, she came rushing back over to where I stood, plotting on the demise of The Hungry Hippo.

"Now, Audie..." she began, placing a hand on my arm, "It's not that deep. You're just stressed out about the upcoming competition and it's making you a little unhinged. Breathe for a second." She spoke slowly and calmly, as if I was a cornered animal getting ready to strike.

"Nah, it's not cool. We're already having trouble bringing people in and then he wants to make it hard for the ones that do come in! I'm not here for it."

"Talk to him later today. Don't make a scene now," she said, waving her hands at the sparse crowd. "It could be bad for business, and we need all the business we can get."

"Fine."

Throughout the night, customers kept coming in to complain about the lack of parking available. Just when I thought I'd gotten to where it didn't piss me off, someone else would come in and make a comment. It was an ugly cycle that everyone was stuck in for most of the shift. Meanwhile, I could see from the window that The Hungry Hippo was booming with customers.

I didn't want to be jealous, but I couldn't help but feel a twinge of it each time I saw people walking into his restaurant in groups. Despite my food being just as good, if not better than his, the difference in our crowds would make you think otherwise. If it kept going this way, Audrey's Kitchen might have to close its doors for good and the thought of that made my heart jump in my throat. I'd do whatever it takes to keep this place open. Even if that meant causing a scene at the competing restaurant because my people had no place to park.

"This food was amazing! Compliments to the chef!" A round man and his friends said to me as they departed. "We'll definitely be back!"

"I'm so happy to hear that. Thank you!" I beamed with pride. Even though I'd been in this business for a minute, I never tired of hearing compliments. It's like crack to a chef. Our egos always needed the boost, at least mine does. And I'm not afraid to admit that.

"My only complaint is the parking." One of his friends said. We nearly turned back because parking was impossible. We had to use one of the spaces down the road a bit."

"I'm so sorry. We're working on it." I replied, trying as hard as I could to remain friendly in the moment, even though I wanted to scream. As soon as they left and we began closing up for the night,

I debated going over there to address the issue with him. The issue may have seemed insignificant, but we were desperate to keep business coming in.

"Overall, we had a really good day today, boss lady." Anika said after we had closed the registers and counted the tills for the night. Her attempt to cheer me up and shift my focus was obvious, but I couldn't stop fixating on the problem.

"Yeah. It could have been better, though."

She sighed, "You're so hard on yourself sometimes, cousin."

"I'm hard on myself because I expect the best. If I don't push myself to be the best, then what's the point?" I repeated the same words my father used to drill into my head constantly when he was alive. "You have to work twice as hard."

"Yeah, yeah, yeah. He was my family, too." Anika replied, rolling her eyes. "I remember what he used to say. He'd be proud of you, you know."

I looked over at her, surprised. "Mom told me that earlier today." I replied quietly.

"Good. You need to remind yourself of that sometimes. Give yourself some grace." She patted my shoulder and then grabbed her keys. "Tell Auntie I said what's up."

I watched her leave, impressed by how much she has grown. For someone so young, she had so much wisdom. Sometimes she seemed light years ahead of me, while I struggled to catch up. I grabbed my things and headed out to my car. I'd told myself that I wouldn't address the parking issue with Montrell, but while I sat in my car, glaring out at his restaurant, it made me angry all over again.

"Get it together, Audrey. You're just stressed." I mumbled to myself, leaning back against my headrest. It wasn't that deep, like Anika had said. I shouldn't let it bother me like this. And even though I knew that, I couldn't shake the feeling that I shouldn't let it slide. If I did, things would continue to happen. This isn't the first time he had passive aggressively messed with my restaurant and if I didn't address it now, it wouldn't be the last time.

With a new resolve, I swung open my car door and slammed it behind me. I had enough time to have a quick conversation with him before I went to the gym. I'd hit the weight machines and cardio to get rid of all this frustration. I stomped over to The Hungry Hippo and swung open the door, determined to give its head chef a piece of my mind.

Chapter Six
Montrell

It was the day before the *Sleigh the Recipe* competition and Jai's incessant chatter about it eroded my enthusiasm. I wasn't interested in participating in this contest. My Christmas wish was to stay home and celebrate with my family. I'd rather listen to Mekhi's boasting about his superior life than be a contestant in this nonsense. Jai, however, was so excited that he couldn't concentrate on anything else most of the day.

He'd purchased extra T-shirts with our Hungry Hippo logo on them and made me promise to wear them during filming. It all felt performative and superficial, but since I had already given him my word that I would win this thing, it felt like I was punking out if I didn't at least try. Even if he was driving me nuts.

"... And make sure the recipes you choose can be ones we can duplicate here. It would be dope to use them to draw in business."

We were closing up the restaurant for the day, and I was doing my best to appear interested in what Jai was talking about. I wasn't succeeding.

"I got it, man." I replied stiffly. Jai's shoulders sagged a bit as my disinterest finally registered.

"I know you're not excited about this, but I promise it's going to be a good thing." He said, clapping his heavy palm against my shoulder. "Think long-term benefits."

I narrowed my eyes at him while he busied himself with flipping the chairs up onto the tables. He could easily be excited because he wasn't involved. Hearing the front door jingle, I realized someone had come in, meaning our server hadn't locked it as instructed. I turned, just in time to see an angry Audrey making her way towards me, her hair swirling around her shoulders as she moved.

"Could you please tell your patrons to stop parking in my empty spaces? It makes it really difficult for my customers to get to the restaurant." Audrey fumed through gritted teeth. I had just stepped over to close out the cash register for the night when she came stomping into my restaurant, clearly looking for a fight.

"Hello, welcome to The Hungry Hippo, unfortunately we are already closed so-"

"I'm not in the mood to play with you, Montrell." She interrupted, narrowing her eyes at me. It took an extraordinary show of strength not to laugh at her irrational anger. Steam practically billowed from her ears like a cartoon character. I wanted to pat her on the head and asked if she'd eaten today, but there was no scenario where that worked in my favor.

"What can I do for you, Ms. Bennett?" I asked, nonchalance dripping from my tone. My calmness seemed to piss her off even more, which I can't help but enjoy just a little. I don't know why I loved getting under her skin so much, but I jumped at any chance to annoy her, just so I could see her get mad at me.

"Have your customers Park. Somewhere. Else." She repeated through gritted teeth, speaking with measured pauses as if I couldn't understand what she was saying.

"My bad. I'll make a sign. Is that all you needed?" I could hear Jai in the back talking to one of the late shift servers. Audrey studied me and then sighed.

"I'm sorry. Stress is really getting to me. I'm in a cooking competition and-"

"Is it *Sleigh the Recipe*?" I asked. Her presence in the competition would add a fun challenge. Audrey was an unstructured mess in the kitchen, but her food was always incredible. I would never dream of telling her that, though. I'd never hear the end of it.

"Yes. How did you know that?"

"Jai signed me up for it the other day." I hadn't expected her to be happy about it, but the look of fury that flashed across her face surprised me.

"Are you serious right now?" She threw her hands up. "First, I can't even have this block to myself and my restaurant. Now you're entering the same competition. Do you have to interfere with everything? Do you always have to be around?"

I put a hand to my chest, feigning hurt. "Your words cut, Ms. Bennett. I'm not even the one that signed myself up for it. We're planning some renovations, and the prize money would really help us out. It was Jai's idea."

"But-" She began and then shook her head. "That's fine. We both know I'm going to win, anyway." Her competitive spirit stirred something in me. This competition no longer seemed like a predictable Christmas money grab.

"Is that a challenge I hear in your voice, Ms. Bennett?" I asked, raising an eyebrow at her. Our eyes locked and something I couldn't read passed through her expression.

"Tell your people to park somewhere else." She turned on her heel and left just as quickly as she had come. I watched as she headed back into her restaurant.

"What was that about?" I had been so wrapped up in Audrey that I hadn't noticed Jai come back in. From the smirk on his face, he had definitely witnessed some of the exchange between us.

"Did you know she was in the competition when you signed me up?" I asked, glancing up at him.

"Nah, man. This was strictly a money move. Why? Does that change your mind?"

The amusement in his tone irritated me, but instead of pushing the issue, I finished up my closing duties and grabbed my gym bag from its spot on the floor in the back office. I couldn't let a day pass without visiting the gym at least once. It's what kept me sane.

"I'm going to the gym to clear my head." I called over my shoulder as I walked to my truck. Jai nodded and headed to his own. I'd offer for him to tag along, but we both knew he wouldn't come. Jai much preferred sitting at home working on a painting or a digital design of some sort.

The gym's parking lot was nearly empty when I got there, with just three other cars. Just the way I preferred it. Everyone else had likely worked out in the morning or throughout the day, leaving the really late gym goers like me with enough space to work out without being interrupted.

My journey to the gym began in high school, a time marked by being overweight and self-conscious about my appearance. I'd grown up hearing some of my classmates refer to me as a Hungry Hippo or start snickering whenever they saw food in my hand and, as a result, I'd developed a lot of shame around eating. I'd begun eating in my car to avoid the stares of others, or fueling myself based on my emotions and not actual hunger. My relationship with food was unhealthy for a long time, a strange fact for a chef and restaurant owner, but taking control finally revealed that food isn't the enemy.

Now, when I'm overwhelmed or full of nervous energy, I come to the gym where I can channel my focus into the weights and in correct lifting form. I locked my car and headed into the gym, my muscles buzzing with pre-workout and anticipation, my favorite combination. I'd just stepped onto the treadmill and settled my headphones over my ears when I glimpsed someone in the mirrors behind me.

Audrey.

I turned, intrigued and annoyed that I couldn't seem to escape this girl. She had changed out of the outfit she had been wearing at work into some leggings that unfairly showcased every curve she had and a crop top. I watched as she readied herself to do a lateral pull-down with an impressive amount of weight loaded onto the machine.

Against my better judgement, I slid my headphones back until they were on my neck and stepped off the treadmill. When I reached her, she glanced up at me and then rolled her eyes. I couldn't help but smile.

"Maybe that stupid thing was right." She mumbled. "What are you doing here?"

I spread my arms out as if the answer was obvious. "This is a gym. I'm working out. What are you doing here this late? You strike me as more of a morning workout type of girl."

"I couldn't make it this morning. Not that it's any of your business." She replied. Her muscles flexed as she pulled the handle of the machine down. I watched silently; a bit impressed by her strength. She wasn't too far behind what I could lift and already way ahead of some of the other men that trained here.

She continued to work out, dismissing me without a word. With a silent nod, I returned to the treadmill, resolutely pushing her from my thoughts. It was a cardio day for me, so I focused all of my energy running. I finished my workout, my shirt drenched and my energy completely depleted.

I scanned the gym, trying to see if she was gone. Besides wanting to annoy her before I left, I couldn't give a reason to look for her. I was sweaty and disgusting, but I still wanted to see her before I headed out. If she hadn't left already. It turns out she hadn't. I spotted her standing just in front of the women's locker room talking to a guy that I had seen a few times in the gym before.

He was tall and lanky, though I could tell from the way he stood he thought he was much more attractive than his appearance warranted. Normally I would go back to minding my business, but something about her body language put me on high alert. She seemed on edge. I took off my headphones as I strolled toward the two of them. The guy hadn't seen me yet, but Audrey saw me coming from over his shoulder.

"I'm saying give me your number and let me take you out sometime." The guy said, stepping closer. Audrey stepped back and folded her arms across her chest.

"I appreciate that, but I'm really not interested." Her tone was polite, but there was a slight sharpness to it, showing that my suspicion had been correct.

"Come on, let me take you out." His persistence was annoying. I could feel myself bristling at his inability to take a hint. Audrey shook her head, her smile still polite, but looking a little more strained.

"You think you're above going out with me?" He demanded.

"No, of course not I- "

"So, stop acting stuck up and just give me your number." His voice had taken on an aggressive tone that didn't sit well with me. I didn't wait for her to give me the go ahead. This guy needed to be dealt with.

"You good?" I asked, looking at Audrey. Her eyes widened, but I held her gaze while I waited for an answer. Out of the corner of my eye, I saw the guy turn to face me, ready to get loud. He squared his stance and puffed out his chest, trying and failing to look intimidating.

"I'm okay." Audrey replied softly. I turned my attention to the guy, unfazed by the fury in his eyes, and scanned the immediate area for anything I could grab if the situation escalated. Whether he knew it, this was not a problem he could handle.

"I believe she said she wasn't interested. Let it go."

"This doesn't involve you, bro," he replied, staring me down. "Her and I were having a conversation."

"I won't repeat myself." I met his gaze with a steely one of my own. Audrey's gasp registered faintly, but I kept my attention focused on the guy in front of me, assessing him. If he made a move, I would be ready for whatever. He could lift. I'd seen him in here before, but he was no match for me. It wouldn't be a fair fight, and if he didn't make a wise choice in the next two seconds, he would see just how unfair that fight would be. His glare lingered for a beat before he deflated, turning away with a mutter about women being self-absorbed and dismissing decent guys.

I waited for him to reach the front door of the gym before turning back to Audrey, who was watching me with an unfamiliar expression. She silently turned and walked into the locker room. When she reappeared a few moments later, a quick wave of relief washed over her face as soon as she spotted me waiting in the same spot she had left me. She tried to mask her relief with the usual annoyed expression she wore whenever she was around me, but I caught it anyway.

"I'll walk you to your car." I said. My tone left no room for debate. The guy was long gone, but I was still seeing red. I surveyed the parking lot as we walked to her vehicle, making sure he didn't decide to circle back. Neither one of us spoke until she pulled her keys out of her bag and clicked the unlock button. The headlights of a dark-colored jeep blinked twice.

"You didn't have to do that." She said finally, looking down at the gravel beneath her feet.

"I absolutely did. Mans wasn't letting up fast enough for me."

"I've never seen you like that before." Her voice was muted, her expression thoughtful. "So... protective. It's nice."

When we locked eyes, something in the air between us shifted. She had moved closer to me, so she had to tilt her head back to meet my eyes. I kept glancing at her full lips, wondering if they were as soft as they looked. I couldn't blame dude for trying to talk to her, she was a gorgeous woman.

"How long you been lifting?" I asked, desperate to change the subject. I needed something to distract myself from the fact that our lips were so close. A slight head dip would be all it took, and here, in this gym parking lot, with adrenaline surging, the temptation proved stronger than expected. Audrey blinked, then cleared her throat and stepped back.

"A few years now."

I nodded, "You're pretty strong."

"Thanks." She smiled softly. We both fell silent, things never feeling this awkward when we were bickering about something. I ran a hand over the back of my neck, searching my brain for something to say but coming up empty.

"You know you're going to lose this competition, right?" Audrey said, smirking up at me. I barked out a laugh, surprised at the sudden change of pace in conversation.

"In your dreams, beautiful. As a matter of fact, go home and get some sleep. You're going to need all of your energy to keep up with me these next few weeks." I made a show of glancing at my watch to see the time.

"You couldn't handle me." Her words were innocent, but I took them in the wrong way. I was struck by the idea of grabbing her thighs and hoisting her up on the hood of my truck. To shake the image from my mind, I shook my head. I just chased away a creep and now here I was, being even worse.

"I'll guess we'll just have to see then."

Chapter Seven
Audrey

Dear Diary,

    The night before the cooking competition, Montrell and Audrey found themselves at the same gym. She was near the locker rooms after he finished his cardio, talking to some guy, but it didn't take long to see that she wasn't interested. The man leaned in closer, ignoring her attempts to brush him off. Montrell didn't hesitate. He walked over, his demeanor calm but protectively watchful. The guy sized Montrell up but eventually backed off, muttering as he walked away. Audrey turned to Montrell; her usual sharpness was momentarily gone. Something about the moment lingered between them.

    By the time they left the gym, something had shifted between them. They both knew it,

even if neither of them was ready to admit it yet. The competition tomorrow was going to be intense, but the real challenge might be figuring out what had just sparked between them.

I read the journal entry that had appeared on the page to my girls, confused on how this thing knew what happened before I told it. Elodie listened with a smug expression, while Monae and Brina said nothing.

"Oh God, Audie, not you too!" she groaned into the phone. We were on our usual Facetime call while I got ready for the first round of the contest, and I had just filled them all in on the journal incident. Since the night I had called Elodie in a panic, it had been producing messages daily. Whenever Montrell and I were together, that annoying journal would blab about it in an entire entry.

"What can I say? You see a journal writing in itself more than once, you become a believer." I glanced at it again, just to make sure it hadn't moved while I wasn't looking. Chili snuggled on my bed while I got ready. Forever the princess with no responsibilities whatsoever.

"I tried to tell y'all." Elodie shrugged, clearly enjoying someone else seeing the magic she'd been convinced of since last year. We all appeased her last year when she endlessly discussed the journal. Now, it's my turn to endure the same treatment.

"I just wish it wouldn't set me with Montrell." I sighed. Their silence prompted me to turn to my phone and face them.

"What?"

"I mean, " Brina began, looking at the others for support. I stopped getting ready, curious to hear what they were all trying so hard not to say.

"We still don't really know why you hate him this much." Elodie finished for her. "Every time he comes over to see us, he's great. He seems like a nice guy." I sat quietly, struggling with trying to explain exactly why I couldn't stand him. I don't think I've ever been able to express how much his words and dismissive behavior towards my passion affected me back then – how it still affects me. I refuse to admit it aloud to anyone; being that vulnerable doesn't suit me. I have to remain confident in my plans, regardless of his opinions. I made it my mission to succeed – to see father's dreams for me through to the end. His carelessness almost cost me my dream and I couldn't forgive that. Could I?

"And he is hot as hell. Have you seen him? It's unfair. He and his brother are gorgeous." Monae was correct. He was handsome. His broad shoulders and sharp jaw made him strikingly handsome. If only he wasn't an arrogant jerk.

"Not too much on my man," Elodie laughed, "But she's right. Both brothers are handsome. Even though I'm partial to Mekhi."

A remarkable personality outweighs a beautiful face. I kept thinking about our encounter at the gym; how quickly he stepped in when he sensed I was uncomfortable, and how he kept looking at me like he wanted to lick the sweat off of my body.

"Whatever you say," Monae shrugged, "Anyway, I've got to go, ladies. My shift starts soon. We've got some extra equipment training coming up that I need to be ready for. Good luck today, Audie!" She waved at us and then clicked out of the conversation. Her departure sparked the rest of us to say our goodbyes and get our days started.

I was supposed to be at the center they were using for the competition in two hours. I'd thought about getting a quick workout session in beforehand to clear my head, but I didn't want to risk being late. My nerves were all over the place about being in front of a camera. The competition was to be filmed live for broadcast the following week, so any mistake I made would be shown to the entire world. No pressure or anything.

I arrived almost two hours early, too anxious to sit in my car and wait, and found the set beautifully decorated. An artificial fireplace covered the far corner of the stage, Christmas stockings with the names of each contestant hung on the mantle of the fireplace. White string lights hung from every surface and a Christmas tree large enough to rival the one in Times Square stood in the middle, covered in ornaments of all shapes and sizes.

"Elodie would absolutely love this." I smiled to myself as I looked around. It felt like stepping into a mini version of a Christmas wonderland - like Hobby Lobby and every other craft store threw up. The back of the room held four small, unused kitchen stations. Each station was fully equipped with a stove, two ovens, a sink, and plenty of cabinets. A massive walk-in pantry occupied the stage's far end, overflowing with every conceivable ingredient.

My anxious nerves gave way to excitement as I took in everything in front of me. Whether or not I won the competition, being able to try new recipes and bring new people into the

Audrey's Kitchen experience was an opportunity I was lucky to have. I made a mental note to call Deja later on and thank her for bullying me into doing this. Without her encouragement, I wouldn't have taken this leap of faith.

"Can I help you?" A small woman, clipboard in hand and a bored look on her face, inquired. I had no idea where she materialized from.

"Hi," I smiled politely, "I'm Audrey Bennett, I'm one of the- "

"A. Bennett? Okay, come with me." She didn't give me a chance to respond before turning on her heels and rushing off behind the stage. I trailed after her until she halted and turned to me, shoving the clipboard in my face. "Sign these forms."

"Oh." I flinched at the sudden change of direction. "Sure." After reading carefully through each one, I signed my name and handed the clipboard back to her with a smile. She didn't return it; instead, she tucked the clipboard under her arm and dashed ahead. When I hadn't moved from my spot, she glanced over her shoulder.

"Are you coming?" She asked, sounding bored. I hurried behind her, unsure of where we were going but too scared to ask questions. The woman led me through the backstage area and through a corridor leading to a small room stocked with water bottles, fruit trays, and a singular television screen on the wall. She pointed to the couch, using her free hand while keeping her eyes on the clipboard.

"Sit here until we're ready for filming. Our makeup specialist will come in and get you ready soon. We have snacks over here while you wait, but we expect your meals to be edible enough for all contestants and the judges to eat to help reduce food waste. What questions do you have for me?" She recited the list without hesitation. I blinked, stunned, and then shook my head.

"None. Thank you."

She nodded and then, just as quickly as she had appeared, she was gone, leaving me to soak up the moment on my own. I settled into the couch and pulled out the journal Elodie had given me. I almost left it home because I was afraid it might act up again, but I brought it at the last minute. Flipping through the journal, I scoffed at the ridiculousness of its entries.

It sounded like my girls, highlighting how attractive he is and how everyone could see the energy between us. Yes, I could see that Montrell was attractive. My eyes worked fine, but ultimately, there were other important factors to consider. Every conversation with him descended into a fight. We had a singular moment at the gym when he had stepped in to help me out, but that was it. I couldn't understand why this magical piece of junk kept trying to convince me he was my soulmate. It was absurd.

A voice on my left remarked, "This place is pretty intense." I glanced up to see a petite blonde woman smiling cheerfully at me. "Hi. I'm Dot. Who are you?"

"I'm Audrey." I smiled back and closed the journal. Dot looked around the room in awe before helping herself to the snack table. My anxiety prevented me from eating, and I didn't enjoy eating from buffets where I couldn't see how the food was prepared or who prepared it.

"Is this your first competition?" Dot asked, mouth full of food.

"Yes, it is. I'm so nervous about being filmed. Do you think many people will watch?" I suddenly felt my hands getting sweaty, remembering that everything would be filmed. It'd be just my luck to face-plant into the floor while I was grabbing ingredients. Dot cocked her head at me and then laughed; the sound similar to someone laughing at a small child or a person they thought stupid.

"Oh honey. It's just going on Facebook live. Nothing serious. This is all incredibly local. Don't worry your pretty little head about that." Her tone was laced with condescension. I was caught off guard by how swiftly she shifted from friendly to patronizing.

"Hello everyone!" A black woman entered, with purple and black braids down to her butt. She smiled at me, nodded briskly at Dot, and then took a seat at one of the tables, not bothering to touch the food.

"I'm Audrey." I greeted from my seat. The woman, smiling again, turned to me. Unlike Dot, it lacked arrogance and condescension.

"Serenity." She replied, glancing around. "I'm so excited to be here. It's a bit of a dream of mine to be in a cooking competition."

"Mine too." Out of the corner of my eye, I could see Dot looking back and forth between the two of us, looking like she wanted to join in, but was unsure of how to insert herself into the conversation. Serenity and I continued to chat while we waited for something to happen. I glanced at the door every few minutes, wondering where our last contestant was. He'd claimed he was competing, too. Did he reconsider at the last moment?

"Are you expecting someone?" Serenity asked, on the millionth time I glanced at the door. I felt my cheeks grow hot with embarrassment.

"No, I-" I began, but the door opening behind me interrupted me. I knew it was him without having to turn around. His presence sucked the air out of the room.

"Wow." Serenity whispered, staring with wide eyes. My hand twitched slightly at her reaction to him and my mind briefly drifted back to the journal before I shook my head, clearing it before I had the chance to spiral.

"Audrey." He said coolly.

"Montrell." I replied, without bothering to turn around. Dot and Serenity looked at him and then looked at me, sensing the sudden elevation in tension. I clamped my lips shut and channeled all of my attention onto my phone, determined not to look up at him.

"Good! Everyone is here!" A guy who looked to be in his mid-fifties with a Santa hat and a sweater covered in Christmas lights and fake snow came bouncing in behind Montrell, capturing our attention. "I'm handling the production, direction, and hosting duties for this event. Since it's such a small production, we all wear a lot of hats. Not just Santa ones!" When no one laughed at his joke, he coughed awkwardly and continued. "Anyway, I'm Rodrigo, and I'm going to go over the rules and expectations with you guys before we get started with the first round. Sound cool?"

"Absolutely!" Dot responded, with way too much enthusiasm.

"Awesome. Okay. So, this is a small local production, so we will broadcast to our fanbase via Instagram and Facebook Live. We want recipes that won't make our audience lose interest, so they need to be fast. There are three rounds. We ask that you all wear these hats to be more festive and in the Christmas spirit." As he talked, the woman that had helped me earlier popped up holding what looked to be elf hats with ears attached. A mortified look passed over Montrell's face, and I couldn't help but laugh at that. I took mine and pushed it down as best as I could over my hair.

"Oh, I love these!" Dot, again; her voice dripping with superficial excitement. If she was this much of a kiss-up during the introductory meeting, I could only imagine how insufferable she'd become when the cameras turned on.

"Great. Okay, we're going to get everyone in makeup and have their mics set up and then we can get this show on the road!"

"Makeup?" Montrell asked, with his brow furrowed.

Rodrigo shrugged as if it wasn't a big deal. "Sure. We need to ensure you look your best under the bright lights. This is Christmas. Not Halloween." With that, he turned on his heels and rushed out of the room.

"I'm going to kill Jai," Montrell grumbled, reluctantly sliding the elf hat on his head. The obnoxious ears jutting from the side made his pouting even funnier. I couldn't wait to talk to my girls tonight and tell them how everything went. After getting our makeup done, we headed to the set where Rodrigo and an entire camera crew waited.

"Beautiful!" Rodrigo clapped his hands excitedly, "Okay everyone, pick a station and we can get started." I chose the kitchen station closest to the Christmas tree, so I could feel like I was home in my kitchen. The only thing I was missing was

Chili laying at my feet while I cooked, hoping to catch a scrap of something as it fell off the counter.

My nerves buzzed excitedly. I couldn't wait to get my hands on the ingredients to cook. As nervous as I was to be filmed, the kitchen was my happy place. I felt the most at home, surrounded by ingredients and elbow deep in some kind of recipe.

"Is everyone ready?" The camera guy asked. Everyone nodded. The competition setup, even though it was only supposed to be streamed online, was impressive. Numerous lights illuminated the set, with cameras positioned at various angles. Even if it wasn't a nationally broadcast show, it certainly felt like it. "Alright. We're live in five...four...three...two...one." He pointed at Rodrigo, who sprang into action.

"Alright! Welcome to *Sleigh the Recipe* everyone! We've got four local chefs and business owners here ready to show us exactly what they can do. The winner will receive ten thousand dollars to go towards their business! Before we get started, let's introduce the contestants." He nodded at me with a big smile. I cleared my throat, praying my voice didn't shake and reveal my nerves to everyone.

"Hi. My name is Audrey Bennett. I am the head chef and owner of Audrey's Kitchen."

"And what gave you the inspiration for Audrey's Kitchen?" Rodrigo asked, steepling his hands and schooling his features into an intense expression.

"Before my father died, he and I used to cook together. It was always my kitchen, he'd say. He was just the sous chef. He was the only one that let me experiment with recipes and ingredients.

Even if it turned out gross."

"That's so touching. Thank you for joining us today. What about you, handsome?" He turned to Montrell with a big smile on his face.

"My name is Montrell Davis. I am the co-owner and head chef of The Hungry Hippo." Montrell deadpanned. It was clear on his face that he didn't want to be here. I resisted the urge to roll my eyes. Rodrigo, however, clapped excitedly, letting out a cackle.

"The Hungry Hippo! That's so interesting. Tell us about the inspiration behind your restaurant!"

"Sure. Growing up, I was a heavier kid, and they used to call me a hungry hippo. It inspired a lot of shame around food and eating for me for a long time, until I went to therapy to rewrite my relationship with food. I learned to cook and opened my restaurant to show people that food isn't the enemy" As he talked, my mind went back to our conversation back in school when he'd first told me about his idea for his restaurant. He'd alluded to being a bigger kid, but he had never gone into detail about how much damage it had caused him. I had to acknowledge their accomplishment. Transforming negativity into positivity was inspiring. From the looks on Serenity's and Dot's faces, they shared similar opinions.

"Oh." Dot breathed, placing a hand over her heart and swiping at a fake tear. "That's so powerful."

"Indeed, it is!" Rodrigo agreed. "To be this gorgeous and inspirational is so unfair!"

Montrell smiled uncomfortably and shrugged. While Dot and Serenity both took turns telling us about their restaurants and the inspirations behind them, I let my mind wander forward, anticipating when we could start. When our gazes met, he made a face and rolled his eyes, prompting a quick smile out of me before I trained my gaze forward. It was game time and I couldn't let him rattle me.

"Okay great! Now that we've met our contestants, let's meet our judges!" Rodrigo waved his hand dramatically to his left, where three people were seated. I had no idea when they managed to sneak in, but they had already made themselves comfortable. Each of them wore a Christmas sweater and a Santa hat to match.

"We have Chef Flamsey, Chef Bordon, and Chef Gemerald! Welcome, welcome!" All three of them waved quickly to the cameras. "Alright. Now that we know everyone, we can get to the fun stuff. The rules are simple. Be quick, be efficient, and be creative! Each round will work together to make one Christmas themed meal. Appetizer, entrée, and dessert. We clear?" He turned back to us with a raised eyebrow. We all nodded, eager to get started.

"Wonderful. This first round is called Holly Jolly Bites! Imagine you just found out guests are coming over and need to whip up a delicious, bite-sized appetizer. You'll find all the necessary ingredients in the pantry. When I say go, you'll have fifty-five minutes to create a masterpiece. Don't let me down!"

I braced myself, ready to take off running towards the pantry as soon as Rodrigo gave the word. My muscles twinged and my mind flooded with excitement. I zeroed in on the goal, letting my mind clear itself of all distractions. I aimed to fully utilize this opportunity. This was going to show everyone that I could hold my own in the kitchen and I couldn't wait to get started.

"On your marks...! Get ready...! Aaaaand... go!"

Chapter Eight
Montrell

Immediately after the host yelled "go," Audrey bolted across the floor to the pantry. I almost wanted to stop and watch her as she raced towards the pantry and started grabbing ingredients like she was on an episode of Supermarket Sweep.

An instrumental version of Jingle Bell Rock played throughout the room while everyone snatched everything they needed to make their dishes. My steps were a little slower, while I debated on which appetizer to make. I was considering two options, and depending on their availability, I'd pick the one that was the quickest to make.

Dot shoved past me, shooting an angry glare over her shoulder as she raced back to her station, her elf ears making her look ridiculous. I shook my head and stepped into the pantry. The food stocked here was incredibly impressive. I could make either dish I had in mind.

While I searched for the items I needed, my elf hat, which I had been forced to wear, slid down on my head, obscuring my vision. Reminding me I needed to cuss Jai out as soon as I could get to my phone. I'd told him from the beginning that I wasn't wearing stupid hats, yet here I was sporting one with obnoxious ears taped to it. I felt like an idiot trying to push it back far enough on my head so it wouldn't fall, but not far enough to take it off. Even though I wanted to toss it into the nearest fire.

After grabbing my ingredients, I headed back to my station to begin the prep. I had opted to make Gougères with smoked salmon, caviar and prosciutto. It's my go-to in party situations because the flavor packs a punch, but they are effortless to make. I preheated my oven and then pulled out a baking sheet so I could line it with parchment paper.

"Oh, this looks fancy. What are you making?" I overheard Rodrigo ask one of the contestants. I chose not to look up and see who he was speaking with. Instead, I heated the water, butter, salt, and pepper in a saucepan for about one minute. The recipe may be simple, but it still involves many steps. I had to make sure to get everything right. If the cream puff dough, that forms the base of the Gougères, didn't cook properly, it would ruin the rest of the process, and I'd have to start over. Winning meant avoiding any mistakes.

"And you, handsome," I'd been so focused, I hadn't noticed Rodrigo making his way over to my station, "What are you making for the judges?"

"Gougères with smoked salmon." I replied, not bothering to

look up. Once I began cooking, there was little that could ruin my focus or steal my attention.

"Pfft. Ambitious." Audrey sniffed. I glanced up, then. Only a brief glance, enough to make her feel my displeasure, before I returned to the cooking. Whatever haphazard disaster she was throwing together was no match for my selection. Rodrigo glanced between the two of us. I felt like I could almost hear the wheels turning in his head as he sensed the tension between us.

"Do I detect a little rivalry here?" He asked, his voice betraying his excitement.

"No, not at all." Audrey deadpanned with a disinterested shrug. I wanted to respond, but I kept going on my dish, refusing to let her nonsense distract me from winning this competition. If I was here and forced to wear Christmas hats against my will, the least I could do was win this round. I transferred the batter I'd made into a pastry bag with a wide tip so I could pipe the dough into one and a half inch mounds on the baking sheet.

As I worked, I was dimly aware of Christmas music playing in the background. It was "The First Noel," a tune my brother insisted on rewriting for his play last year. I smiled to myself as I remembered how he obsessed over making sure everything was flawless. My brother treated music the way I treated food. Everything needed to be precise in order to create a masterpiece.

I topped each dough mound with Gruyere cheese. One of my favorites. It had a creamy texture with a mild nutty flavor. Nothing too crazy, but it elevated whatever dish it was a part of. Once topped, I placed the dough in the oven to bake for about twenty minutes. While that baked, I prepared the salmon and the caviar to go on top. I had plenty of time to spare.

"Forty minutes left, dearies!" Rodrigo announced, clapping his hands together excitedly, "I can't wait to taste these delicious treats!"

Despite my initial reluctance, the thrill of preparing a dish under pressure was invigorating. It coursed through me, giving me a surge of energy. It was similar to the busy days in the restaurant, where multiple dishes needed to be prepared in a satisfactory time frame. I thrived under that type of pressure. Though I'd never tell Jai, I'm grateful he convinced me to enter the competition. I was having fun.

When the Gougères were ready to come out of the oven, I grabbed my oven mitt. I glanced up, catching Audrey's eye and her weird expression, only to realize I had been swaying along to the music. I cleared my throat and straightened, feeling a twinge of embarrassment. Cooking put me in a good mood and when I was in a good mood, I was always lighter on my feet.

I had my dish plated and ready to go with time to spare. It gave me a few moments to sit back and observe the competition. Dot was flitting around her station, pulling out pots and pans, looking like she wanted to sit in the middle of the floor and pull her hair out. Serenity moved to the music, a smile on her face, finishing her dish. Then my gaze drifted to Audrey. I caught her just as she finished plating the last dish, a smile on her face as she stepped back. She looked like she had just accomplished her life goal with that one dish. From where I stood, it seemed impressive, yet it paled compared to my creation. The judges were going to love it. This ten thousand would come home with me.

"Okay lovelies! That's time!" Rodrigo yelled from where he had been chatting with the judges. I had to give it to him and his crew. He'd meticulously thought of every detail to make this competition seem as legitimate as he could by modeling the set and the rules after some of the more popular game shows. It felt like I was on the set of The British Bakeoff, a show I watched whenever I needed some inspiration.

"Oh, no!" Dot cried, "I'm not done! This is so unfair! Please! I'm not finished yet!"

"Plate what you have, dear." Rodrigo replied, unmoved by her exclamation.

"But!" She began, tears streaming down her cheeks. "It's not finished." I'd seen the smug look she'd worn while we waited for the first round to start. Seeing her looking mortified and defeated brought me a small sense of joy. I locked eyes with Audrey, just in time to see her smug smile, before it disappeared.

"Alright everyone. We'll give Dot a minute to collect herself, and then we will have you tell us about your yummy treats! I'm so glad I wore my stretchy pants today!" I resisted the urge to roll my eyes at Rodrigo and instead focused my attention on the judges. If you paid attention to the culinary world, you knew exactly who they were. They were three well-known chefs from different specialties, each a pioneer in the field. Being able to cook for them was an honor, even if by some ridiculous chance I didn't win.

After Dot stopped sniffling and plated what she had, we all stepped out from behind our stations and waited for the judges to approach. They went to Dot first. The trio stood in front of her station, unsympathetic, as they awaited her explanation of the dish.

"Tell us what you have, Dot." Rodrigo said, in a noticeably less eager tone.

"I made eggplant chips." She said, hanging her head, "But I ran out of time, so they aren't crispy like I had planned for them to be."

"Time management is important," Chef Flamsey said, looking down her nose at the plate Dot handed her. The poor woman's cheeks turned a bright red with shame. I wanted to look away out of second-hand embarrassment, but it was like watching a train wreck. I couldn't tear my eyes away from the disaster unfolding in front of me. Chef Flamsey cut into the still very tough piece of eggplant and narrowed her eyes.

"This is completely raw." She sniffed, looking back up at Dot, whose eyes widened.

"I-well... these stove jets. Something's gotta be wrong with them because-"

"Nonsense." Rodrigo interrupted, offended, "I made sure my chefs had all the best equipment."

The other two judges put their plates down and, without a word, all three of them moved to the next station, leaving Dot hanging her head in shame. The elf ears on her Christmas hat making the entire thing look a little more comical than it should.

"Serenity, dear. Tell us what you made!"

Serenity nodded, a bright smile on her face. "I made my famous Spinach and Artichoke dip! It's something that my mom absolutely loves to get at Red Lobster, so I learned how to make my version of it." She leaned forward in a conspiratorial whisper. "Mom likes mine better."

That earned a chuckle out of the judges as they lifted the plates closer to their faces. Serenity crossed her fingers behind her back, a silent prayer for positive results, but otherwise kept her facial expression neutral. I appreciated her poker face. Never let them see you sweat.

"This is very good." Chef Flamsey nodded, taking another bite.

"Incredibly flavorful." Chef Bordon chimed in.

"However, it's not very original." Serenity's face fell for a split second before she smiled brightly and nodded.

"Thank you for your feedback." The judges smiled at her and then headed to my table. I was confident in my dish, but the unforgiving way they judged Dot and Serenity made me a little nervous.

"Montrell, you know the drill." Rodrigo said.

"I made Gougères with smoked salmon, caviar and prosciutto." I handed each judge a plate. As I watched them study my dish, I attempted to keep my features neutral, even though I could feel my earlier confidence fading.

"Presentation is decent." Chef Flamsey said, turning the plate around to look at it from the other side. The other two chefs nodded in agreement. I held my breath in anticipation as the three of them took a bite of the dish. A heavy silence descended as all three judges chewed.

"The flavor is lovely."

"And the presentation is simple, yet elegant."

I breathed a sigh of relief. It was a good guess that Dot was the one not making it to the next round of the competition, but you never could tell. After finishing their plates, the judges moved on to Audrey's station. Once my turn was done, I had a chance to check out her dish. As much as I hated to admit it, she had created something impressive.

"Audrey, dear, you know the drill!" Rodrigo said with a flourish of his hands. She smiled and nodded. I listened to her every word, captivated by the way she commanded the room while she talked.

"I made Toasted Ravioli with Marinara Sauce."

"What made you pick this as your dish?" Chef Gemerald asked, looking genuinely curious.

Audrey shrugged. "Who doesn't love fried cheese?"

"Why are they green?" Rodrigo peeked over Chef Flamsey's shoulder to get a closer look.

"I used a bit of natural green food coloring so that way I could arrange them to look like a Christmas tree with little dollops of sauce as the ornaments. In the spirit of the holiday and all."

"I absolutely love the presentation!" Chef Bordon took a bite. His eyes rolled in the back of his head. "This is delicious." The smile that spread on Audrey's face made me want to smile as well.

"I didn't have the chance to make the ravioli by hand with the time constraints, but I used a special ingredient." She explained, beaming with pride.

"Wonderful!"

"I had to improvise," she shot a pointed look in my direction, "But it came out great! Thank you so much for the opportunity!"

"Time for the judges to deliberate!" Rodrigo announced. All three judges stepped to the side and huddled together. I wanted to laugh at how seriously they were taking this entire thing, but I pressed my lips together. While the judges talked, Dot came stopping over and folded her arms.

"This is an unfair contest!" She whined.

"You didn't manage your time correctly, so now the entire contest is unfair?" Serenity asked, tilting her head. Dot's cheeks flushed an angry shade of crimson.

"The stovetop is broken!"

"You don't even know if you've lost yet." Audrey shrugged. Serenity whipped her head around in her direction, disbelief coloring her features.

"Her eggplant was raw! Come on now."

"Weirder things have happened."

Before anyone could respond, the judges stepped back from their huddle and turned towards us. Nervousness stiffened my shoulders for a moment. I could no longer deny I cared about this competition in a way that I didn't expect - stupid hats and Christmas music aside. Being able to share my craft with the world was an amazing opportunity. Despite local filming, competition videos frequently went viral online. Something that was only supposed to be broadcasted to the local community could end up on the other side of the world by tomorrow.

"Alright my lovelies! Gather around!" Rodrigo waved us all back to our stations. Chef Flamsey glanced at the other guest judges before turning to address the four of us.

"As you know, creativity, presentation, and taste are the three key ingredients of this challenge. With that being said, Dot? Could you step to the front, please?" Dot stepped forward on shaky legs.

"Not only was your dish incomplete, it was raw. That's simply not acceptable in the kitchen. Please grab your knives, you will not make it to round two." Tears coated in mascara streamed down her cheeks as she packed her things and headed back to the dressing room. Her sobs echoed from the hallway as she left, determined to make her exit as dramatic as possible.

"Alright. All three of your dishes were delicious, but one of you really outshined in presentation, flavor, and ingenuity."

Audrey threw a look at me, her expression unreadable. I studied her for a moment, wondering what she was thinking, then turned back to the judges, eager to hear who had won. Even if I didn't win this round, there were still two others for me to come out on top.

"Don't keep us in suspense, Judges!" Rodrigo exclaimed, bouncing on his toes excitedly. Chef Flamsey smiled at him, then turned to the cameras in the room — cameras I'd nearly forgotten were there. They'd stayed out of the way while capturing the entire event from multiple angles. I wondered if they caught Dot pushing her way past me out of the pantry, or the looks Audrey and I kept exchanging whenever I glanced in her direction. I couldn't figure out why my eyes kept drifting over to her, even when I was focusing on cooking. The fact that she could catch my attention with her comments earlier says a lot. I'm rarely distracted from my cooking.

"The winner of the Holly Jolly bites round for the most creative, most presentable, and most edible dish is...!

Chapter Nine
Audrey

"Audrey Bennett!" The judges clapped after Chef Flamsey announced my name. My knees threatened to buckle under me. I was proud of my dish, but I hadn't expected to win. Tears threatened to spill down my cheeks, but I blinked them away. I smiled so hard my cheeks hurt. This was just the first round. I had two more rounds to go.

"Congratulations, Audrey! You've won the first round! As your prize, you get to take home this gorgeous solid gold standing mixer, donated to us by Grocery Pro!" As Rodrigo talked, one of the crew wheeled out a completely gold standing mixer. It far surpassed the condition of my standing mixer, a constant victim of my culinary experimentation. I had been meaning to replace it, but hadn't gotten around to it.

"Thank you so much!" I gushed.

"Congratulations, beautiful! You did that!" Serenity exclaimed, hugging me around the neck. I hugged her back, so grateful for what felt like a truly joyous reaction from her, even though she had lost the first round.

"Thank you!" I couldn't control the wide smile that spread across my face.

The next round will begin at the end of this week. Until then, take whatever food items you'd like out of the pantry. We will restock the pantry next week in time for the second round of the competition. Drive safe, my babies!" With a dramatic wave of his hands, Rodrigo exited the stage. The camera crew began shutting down their equipment. The assistant from earlier materialized, out of thin air, and directed us toward the pantry.

"There are reusable shopping bags in the corner." She announced, with the same amount of unenthusiasm as earlier, "Go nuts."

Serenity looped her arm through mine. "I saw a jalapeno jam in here that I am dying to try!"

She dragged me into the pantry with her. While I was searching for the ingredients for my appetizer, I had seen a few items I'd like to try for myself. My gaze scanned the room, looking for Montrell. The round's end brought the journal and its subject back to the forefront of my thoughts. I stepped over to the jams while Serenity read the labels on a few of them.

"So, how long have you been cooking?" I asked, looking at the label of the bacon, gouda jam. It sounded like it would taste good. Who didn't like bacon and cheese? I couldn't decide what it should be on, but I slid it into my bag anyway. During the first round, she'd mentioned always being involved in her family's restaurant business, but never mentioned when she'd started in the kitchen.

"For most of my life. My sisters and I would cook dinner for the family on days when our parents were busy with the business." She grabbed an extra jar of jalapeno jam.

"Do you enjoy working for your family?"

"Honestly?" She grabbed a few blocks of cheese. "I've been searching for a way to leave for a while now. My family is incredibly important to me, but they are slaves to tradition. I want to branch out and try new things. Cooking is art, and its artistry can speak to all five senses. I feel like my family boxes themselves in with their refusal to explore."

"You ever considered opening your own spot?" I took two cartons of eggs and a box of whole wheat pasta. Serenity's face balled up like I asked her if she had licked the floor. I raised an eyebrow, shocked by her reaction.

"No. I don't want the responsibilities of running the business. I'm looking to be part of a fantastic team."

Montrell entered the pantry, interrupting me as I was about to respond. He had stepped away to make a phone call after the competition had ended. For a second, I thought he wasn't going to take advantage of the free food they were offering. Annoyingly, his presence sent a flood of calm through me I couldn't explain.

"Hey." He said, nodding at me.

"Hi." I replied.

"Congratulations on winning. The ravioli Christmas tree was a nice touch." He gave me a lazy, lopsided grin.

"Thank you." I smiled politely. "Yours was a nice try." He narrowed his eyes at me for a second, then shook his head and went back to examining the shelves.

"What is the deal with you two?" Serenity whispered.

"I don't know what you mean."

"Girl please, the sexual tension is thick enough to cut with one of these butcher knives in here!" Her whisper was loud enough to get Montrell's attention. He looked at the two of us, curious.

"Hush!" I snapped. "There is no sexual tension. You're clearly just imagining things." My mind drifted back to the journal waiting inside my bag in the dressing room. It would most likely have another entry in it when I picked it back up again. Something else to try to convince me I belonged with Montrell Davis.

Serenity studied me for a moment, then nodded. "Ah. You're still in the denial phase of this whole thing. Say less. I'll play along."

I glared at her, searching for something to say but coming up with nothing that would persuade her. I glanced back at Montrell to see if he was still listening, but he had busied himself with searching through the different frosting flavors; he was squinting at a peppermint chocolate chip.

"There is nothing going on between me and Montrell, girl. I promise. As a matter of fact, are you interested? I saw you gawking at him earlier. I can introduce you."

"Mhm. I'm not getting mixed up in that." Serenity smirked at me. I sighed and turned back to the shelves, determined not to let his presence ruin the moment for me.

"So how did the first round go?! Tell me everything!" Deja gushed. I'd called her as soon as I got home.

"I won. They gave me a really pretty stand mixer." I replied, glancing at the box I had just sat on my counter. I couldn't wait to crack it open and start making things, but right now, my body was exhausted. Filming had taken most of the day. We had to film the competition itself, and then they also asked us to shoot green screen moments. It felt as close to a real cooking show as you could get, just without the famous hosts.

By the time I had dragged myself back to my apartment, I was ready to rip my clothes off and plunge into bed. Chili welcomed me at the door, delighted to see me after a long day. While I filled Deja in on what happened, I replenished Chili's food and gave her clean water. She happily slurped away while I leaned against the counter.

"That's awesome, Audie! I knew you'd do well at this thing." I stayed silent, chewing on my bottom lip. "Why don't you seem excited?"

"This whole journal thing is really getting to me." I finally sighed, feeling slightly embarrassed. "It's getting in my head. Now, every time he gets near me, I freak out, wondering if it could be right. It was so much easier to hate him when I didn't have this journal in the back of my mind."

"You're still worried about that?" Deja asked, sounding like I was wasting my time even thinking about it. I glanced over at Chili, who was devouring her food, and shrugged even though Deja couldn't see me.

"You'd be worried too if a haunted journal was telling you that your soulmate was someone you couldn't stand!"

She snorted a laugh. "Haunted? Girl, come on. It's not haunted."

"Explain the mysterious entries, then. I'm not writing it and unless Chili grew thumbs when I wasn't looking, there's no one else in the house that could have done it." I was growing irritated with not being believed. Now I understood how Elodie must have felt, and I hated it. I wish I could turn back the time and be on her side when she was venting to us about her situation.

"I'm sorry. I don't mean to laugh. This whole thing is pretty unbelievable, you have to admit."

Despite her valid point, I was still annoyed. I should have called Elodie instead. I glanced at the time displayed on the microwave. It was still early enough to call her without disrupting her sleep.

"It's fine. I'll talk to you later. I've got to get ready for work tomorrow."

After hanging up with Deja, I quickly dialed Elodie's number. She picked up on the third ring, sounding a little winded. I could hear grunting in the background. My eyes grew wide.

"Hello?" She asked, huffing loudly.

"Elodie, did you answer the phone in the middle of you

hunching?!" I hissed, mortified that she would do something so wild. Me and my girls were close, but not close enough to hear each other have sex. That was strictly off limits.

"What?" Elodie asked and then laughed, "No! Of course not. I challenged Kellan and Mekhi to a Zumba competition. Hang on."

I heard rustling, followed by silence, before Elodie spoke again. When she did, her voice was much clearer.

"What's up? How did the first round go?"

"It went well. I won. Listen... did your grandmother ever tell you how this journal started writing in itself?" As I talked, I grabbed it out of my bag and tossed it onto the bed. The pages fluttered as it landed with a soft thump.

"She wasn't much help with that. It was passed down in my family for generations."

"But we aren't related, though," I sighed. "I'm trying to figure out why it's me. Why not Javon, your actual sibling?"

"Why not you?" She asked. "If it's your turn for a little extra happiness this year, why fight it?"

I didn't have an answer. She was right, but what everyone seemed to overlook was that my frustration stemmed from the fact that the journal wasn't setting me up with a knight in shining armor. It's Montrell Davis. The source of my misery in culinary school and over the last couple of years of Audrey's Kitchen.

"Did the journal have another entry tonight?" Elodie asked, breaking the tense silence. I flipped it open and to the last page, feeling nervous about what I would find. Another entry, in the same handwriting, was right there. Something more recent. I let out a shaky breath and swallowed.

"Yes. There is another entry."

"Well. Read it out loud! What does it say?" She asked, barely concealing the excitement. I took a deep breath and read.

Dear Diary

It's funny how life has a way of bringing people together, even when it seems impossible. Montrell and Audrey had a falling out years ago — a misunderstanding so big, it felt like their paths would never cross again. They stopped speaking, both too proud to acknowledge what had transpired between them and went their separate ways. But destiny had other plans.
Here they are, years later, stuck in the same competition cooking side by side. The unspoken tension lingers, but the passion they both share for cooking is thawing the old bitterness. Soon, they'll realize that the misunderstanding wasn't as important as the connection they've created. Perhaps they were destined to be together, united by the same force that had driven them apart — food. It feels like fate knew they needed time to grow apart, only to come back stronger, together.

After I finished reading, I fell silent. My heart hammered in my chest. Cooking is easing the old bitterness. Fate knew they needed time to grow apart. None of it felt right. The story didn't feel like it was truly about Montrell and me, because if it was, they'd know it was more than just a silly misunderstanding. His carelessness put my entire career on the line before I even got started. I had to fight and scrape my way back to a good place thanks to his arrogant and mean-spirited actions. I couldn't forgive that.

Six Years Earlier

"I have received and graded your proposals. If you're here, that means you have passed the final assignment thus far. Now it's time for the second step of the process. To create." Our instructor walked through the small walkway in between our cooking stations, looking each one of us in the eye. Montrell and I stood shoulder to shoulder, awaiting our instructions.

My nerves buzzed with excitement. This was my final step in the entire course. I would be done. I could finally call myself a trained chef. A dream that I had been holding on to since I was a small child was finally becoming reality. I glanced up at Montrell, expecting to see similar excitement on his face, but instead was met with an icy glare. His body was tense, his shoulders impossibly rigid. He looked like he wanted to be anywhere but here. My brows furrowed, trying to silently ask him what was wrong. He shook his head and looked away from me, the muscles in his jaw flexing.

Instead of allowing myself to obsess about why he was acting weird, I turned my attention back to the instructor. I'm sure whatever he had an attitude about was something silly. Maybe one of his many girlfriends broke up with him or something.

"Bennett and Davis, you two will be going first. You'll have two hours to come up with something to serve the judges. The rest of you are dismissed for the time being. Your cook times will be announced via email. Good luck." The rest of our classmates dispersed, leaving Montrell and I alone to discuss.

"What's wrong with you?" I asked, folding my arms, "Girlfriend didn't kiss you goodbye today?" Montrell glared at me, looking like he would rather chew gravel than to be standing in this room with me right now. I felt a twinge of embarrassment, under his scrutinizing gaze. We usually had a back-and-forth thing going. His silence was unsettling.

"I'm fine. Let's just get this started." He grumbled, glancing away from me. I stared at him for a minute, trying to swallow my hurt. I didn't do anything to him, so I couldn't understand why he was being so hateful.

"Alright. Whatever you say."

We prepared the dish in silence. He was in charge of cleaning the meat and the vegetables, while I prepared the rest. His sullen mood threw me off my game completely, but I did my best to readjust and refocus. I couldn't let him ruin what I had worked so hard to achieve.

After everything was plated and ready for the grading panel, I shot one last look at Montrell, hoping that maybe his mood had cleared, but he stared straight ahead, refusing to look at me. The first judge sliced into her chicken and took a bite, the next judge took a bite, followed by the last one.

"This chicken is..." one began, and then made a disgusted face. My heart sank.

"Raw. It's absolutely raw!"

"Raw chicken?" The instructor turned to us, a look of disappointment on his face. "Absolutely unacceptable. Chefs, please leave the room for a moment while we decide what to do." I opened my mouth to protest, but nothing came out. My heart began to thud, and my vision tunneled as panic set in deep in my bones. I would never feed them raw chicken. I may not be the perfect chef, but that was one thing I would never do. This can't be right.

"Hang on. Can I speak to you privately for a moment?" Montrell finally spoke up, after spending the entire experience sullen and quiet. The instructor nodded. I watched, frozen in place, as Montrell stepped away from me. I strained to hear their whispers, feeling my heart sink even further the longer their conversation took.

"Davis and Bennett, I will give you a few moments to discuss how you'll plead your case." He began, folding his arms, "As you know, this assignment makes up the majority of your final grade. I'm sorry, but you cannot turn in raw food. We will proceed with the rest of the class assignments. I expect you two in my office as soon as this is over."

Tears welled up in my eyes. I stared at Montrell, hurt and shocked that he would stoop let me down when I counted on him the most. After all of his ranting about how my menu wasn't good enough and how I'd never be successful doing things the way I had planned, he ended up being the one that couldn't rise to the occasion. He avoided my gaze while we headed out of the room.

"How could you?" I hissed once we had stepped out of the class.

"It's fine. I'll fix it. Just let me talk to the professor." He leaned against the wall looking unbothered, while my dream began to crack down the middle like an overcooked cheesecake.

Later that evening, after the last group presented their dish and class concluded for the day, I walked on shaky legs to the professor's office. I had no idea what to do other than to beg on my hands and knees for another shot.

Montrell was already there, waiting outside when I arrived. Anger swelled up inside of me at the sight of him standing there looking unbothered by the entire situation. I wanted to slap that smug expression off his face. When his gaze landed on me, something in his gaze shifted. He opened his mouth to say something, but the door to the office swung open before he could.

"Bennett." The professor's tone was clipped and dripping with disapproval. "Come in."

The door closed behind me with an ominous click. My palms began to sweat, and I could feel my vision begin to tunnel. Being in this office, scrambling for something to say to convince him that I still deserved to pass after failing so miserably made my insides hurt. I had never been in the position to have to beg for my grade. I'd always excelled in school. Until now.

"I've already spoken with Davis, and he explained to me what happened."

My mouth went dry. "What did he say?"

"He informed me that the recipe was too complex for the amount of time allotted. But you'd insisted on following through with it anyway."

"He said it was my fault?" My voice came out in a strained squeak. I struggled to contain the anger surging through me. Instead of owning up to his mistake, he decided to throw me under the bus all on my own. This was how he had planned to fix it? The instructor watched me closely, studying my face. His eyes focused so intently on me made me nervous, but I pushed it aside and squared my shoulders, determined to do whatever it took to get through this.

"What are my options?"

"You can repeat the entire semester," his gaze flickered toward the door, "Or there is something else you can do."

"What is it? Tell me. I will do whatever it takes." I could hear the desperation in my tone. Part of me felt embarrassed at how pathetic I sounded but the other part, the louder part, couldn't fail. I've never failed.

"Listen, I see how badly you want this. And I am willing to overlook this grade if you're... willing to do something for me in return."

"Something like what?" I asked, confused. He remained silent, staring at me, waiting for me to catch on. I stared back, lost, until it clicked. "Are you asking me to-"

"You're incredibly beautiful. We're both consenting adults.

It's not unheard of." He shrugged, seeming bored with the conversation. Bile rose in my throat, threatening to spill out of my mouth. I'd looked up to this man, soaking in every word and every piece of advice like it came from God himself. To be put in this position, with my dream hanging in the balance, made me want to scream. It made me want to break something. It made me want to wrap my hands around his throat and squeeze until-

"No." I choked out. "No. Absolutely not."

He stared at me for a moment and then nodded curtly. "I'll see you next semester, then."

I turned and rushed out of the room before my brain could catch up to what was happening. I had to get out of that office and away from that man. I stumbled into the hallway and directly into Montrell, who had been waiting in the same spot he'd stood when I'd first went inside. Only a few minutes had passed, but that was all it took for my world to be tilted on its axis. Montrell glanced up from the phone he had been scrolled on and stepped forward, reaching for me.

"Let me explain." He began, but I held my hand up. I didn't want to hear anything he had to say to me at this moment or ever again. "Audrey, please. I didn't mean for this to happen. You have to believe me."

"No! You selfish bastard! Everything I have been working towards is on the line because of you!" Tears slipped down my cheeks. I swiped at them angrily and turned away. "Please just leave me alone. You got what you wanted."

"Hey, are you okay? Why are you crying?" He asked, placing his hands on my shoulders to look me in the eye. I snatched away from his grip, feeling sick to my stomach and desperate to hide from the world.

"Leave me alone, Montrell." I hissed.

He hesitated for a moment, looking like he was debating going against my wishes. I swung back around and glared at him, tears still running down my cheeks.

"Fine." He replied and then left, leaving me to face my crumbling chef career all on my own.

Chapter Ten
Montrell

Despite the early hour, my eyes snapped open. I hadn't been able to get much sleep, no matter how hard I tried. Today marked the second round of the competition, and I was ready to give it my all. Audrey had won the first round, and I couldn't deny that she deserved it. Even though I'd put a lot of effort into my dish, she had gone above and beyond in the creativity department. I'd wanted to congratulate her in depth, but she had been so wrapped up in talking with the other contestant, Serenity, that I didn't want to interrupt.

I had been hoping that we could call a truce somehow. Frankly, I was tired of arguing, but every time I talk to her, she gives me the cold shoulder. Our most recent attempt at a conversation happened the other night at the gym. I had been looking for her every day since, hoping to catch her mid workout, but she was excellent at avoiding me when she wanted.

Seeing my brother and his ready-made family had me in my feelings more than usual. Last night, they came by to offer good wishes and help me forget about the competition. Seeing the way Mekhi and Elodie moved together, so in sync, had made me entertain the idea of calling my ex just for some company. Thankfully, I'd talked myself out of that guaranteed headache. She was the last thing I needed.

When I made it to the building where the competition was happening, Audrey was the only one there, aside from the camera crew. I had expected Serenity to be here already, talking her ear off, so when I saw her sitting by herself reading an unmarked book, I couldn't help but approach her.

"What are you reading?" I asked, walking up to her. She leaped out of her skin at the sound of my voice and shoved the book back in the bag, sitting at her feet. Her reaction surprised me. "Stealing recipes?"

"No," she said, her response a little too quick. "Of course not. What do you want, Montrell?"

I resisted the urge to smile at her curt response. "Can we talk?"

She didn't respond, and I took her silence as a cue to keep going. I took a seat next to her, the warm vanilla of her perfume tickling my nose.

"Look, I know we don't have the best history." I hesitated, running a hand over the back of my neck. That was an incredibly understated way to put it. My actions sabotaged her final assignment in school and made her repeat a semester. At the time, I'd thought my explanation was valid, but she hadn't given me the opportunity to say it. Now, years later, it felt stupid and instead of apologizing like a grown man, I let distance and misunderstanding increase the rift between the two of us. It was a cowardly move.

She stared at me, her brown eyes full of disapproval. "That's putting it mildly, don't you think?"

"You're right." I laughed nervously. Being this close to her made my mind flash back to seeing her in the gym. Her lateral muscles flexing as she used the pull-down machine. We'd shared a moment, however fleeting, and I'd been thinking about it off and on ever since. I wanted more than just the constant arguing and the cold shoulder with her. If I'm honest with myself, I'd wanted more since I met her back in school, but I let our wildly different cooking styles fuel my decision to keep my feelings to myself. After that dreaded final exam, she'd made it clear that she wanted nothing to do with me. Even years later, after she had graduated and moved on from culinary school, her hatred for me never seemed to fade, not even with time. She wanted nothing to do with me and that was a horrible feeling, so I kept my thoughts to myself and gave her space. It was a dumb reason to be dishonest with someone. I was aware of that now.

"Do you want to get something to eat with me after this?" I blurted.

"What?" She was rightly surprised. I wanted to come clean and explain everything, but I didn't want to do it here, with the threat of Serenity or even Rodrigo bursting through the door at any moment. I wanted us to have privacy.

"You and me? Getting something to eat. You eat, don't you?" She rolled her eyes at my comment; a smile pulling at the corners of her mouth.

"Sure. I guess." She replied with a shrug. I saw her gaze flicker back to the book she had shoved in her bag.

"Great. Good luck today." Serenity burst into the room, a flurry of colorful braids and matching glasses. Audrey's expression lit up as soon as she saw her. I smiled to myself, watching the two of them giggle and whisper to each other like high schoolers. Audrey's agreement to go out with me excited me, although I was curious about what caused her change of heart. Usually, she wanted nothing to do with me, but instead of fixating on that, I channeled my energy into this next round of the competition. Two more rounds and then this thing would be over. I will have fulfilled my best friend duties to Jai and could go back to my life's regularly scheduled programming.

"Hello my lovelies!" Rodrigo's singsong voice rang through the room before he'd fully entered. I shook my head; the man was built for show business. His glittery green and red tuxedo made him look like a walking Christmas ornament. As soon as he was on stage under the lights, he'd be blinding. "Are we ready to get started?"

"Let's get you guys dressed!" He flicked his wrist and the woman from the first day somehow materialized next to him, holding three equally glittery Santa Hats. I glared, annoyed that I'd have to wear another obnoxious hat. Excess glitter rained down from the hats with each movement. I'd be wiping glitter off of myself for the next three weeks. "No need for explanations. You have all been here before."

When we all lined up at our stations, ready for instructions,

Rodrigo hopped back into host mode immediately, turning towards the camera with a dramatic sweep of his arms. "Welcome to round two of *Sleigh the Recipe*! I am your host, Rodrigo, and these are our lovely chefs. To our right, we have our judges." The same three judges from the first round waved at the cameras.

"Alright. Before we get started. Tell me. What is your favorite Christmas movie?" He asked, pointing at Audrey. She smiled and chewed on her bottom lip, contemplating.

"I would have to say the new Jingle Jangle movie. It's become an annual tradition for me to watch it."

I hadn't seen Jingle Jangle yet, but the way Mekhi described the music arrangement and the underrated storyline made it sound good. He rarely gave in to the cheesy hallmark vibes of Christmas movies.

"Good choice. What about you, handsome?" He asked, turning to me.

"Um... the Grinch Stole Christmas?" I replied with a shrug. "He was misunderstood for most of the movie. He made some stupid decisions out of hurt, but everyone realized he just wanted to be included. He wasn't so bad after that." It was Kellan's favorite movie and the first one that popped in my mind. He loved to imitate the Grinch's sneaky tip toe. He failed miserably, but his attempts were entertaining to watch.

Audrey snorted, "Of course."

"And you, doll?" Rodrigo turned to Serenity, who had been so quiet I'd forgotten she was even there. She flashed a perfectly white smile at the camera.

"The Christmas Carol."

"Oh! That's another great one!" Rodrigo exclaimed, clapping his hands together. "Alright, let's get to the good stuff. This round is called Merry Mains. You are to create an entrée for the judges that is full of Christmas cheer, and let's make sure it's cooked all the way through, yes?"

I couldn't help but smile at his reference to Dot, who was probably somewhere screaming into a pillow about how unfair the contest was. My muscles twitched with excitement. The first round had been a chance to feel out the competition and see what I was getting myself into. I understood my opponents better now. A mischievous grin spread across Rodrigo's face as he looked at the three of us.

"Okay! Shoo! Shoo! Go cook!" He waved his hands and the three of us took off towards the pantry, eager to get started. I planned to make my famous Glazed Honey Balsamic Pork Chops with roasted garlic parmesan potatoes. It was a recipe I'd stolen from my mother and given my spin. Every year for Thanksgiving, she would break out the different meats and cook them in fancy ways. This was one of the first dishes I was determined to learn how to make when I started to appreciate food.

The smells from all three of our stations combined to make a mouthwatering aroma. My stomach growled while I cooked and, as tempted as I was to sample as I went, I refrained from eating any of the food. While I seasoned the pork chops and then dredged them in flour to sear them in my saucepan, my mind drifted back to the conversation Audrey and I had before this round started.She'd agreed to go grab dinner with me. I was caught off guard when she said yes, so I had no clue where to take her. I never thought I'd reach this point. My gaze drifted to her station; Briefly, I wondered what it would feel like to have her full attention on me. To be the one she handled with such care and focus. I blinked, shocked by the thought, then shook my head. I had a competition to win.

"What are we making?" Rodrigo asked, tilting forward to see inside my saucepan.

"Glazed Honey Balsamic Pork Chops with Garlic Parmesan Potatoes." I replied, laughing at his expression.

"My goodness, that sounds amazing! Save some for me, dear."

"I'll let you have a taste." I grinned at him and winked. We both whipped around when a loud clatter drew our attention to Audrey just as her bowl of utensils crashed to the floor. She snatched them up and smiled, her cheeks flushed. Had she heard me?

"I- sorry!" She exclaimed, eyes wide. "I dropped my um... I dropped my thing."

"I bet." Serenity giggled. Audrey glared at her. I looked back and forth between the two of them, wondering what I was missing. Serenity was aware of something I wasn't. Did I say something wrong?

"What are you making, doll?" Rodrigo redirected the conversation with ease. I saw him, out of the corner of my eye, sauntering over to Audrey's station to check out what was in her skillet. "It smells absolutely divine."

"Spinach and Mushroom Stuffed Tenderloin." She replied. A sound choice. I could tell she was smiling proudly, without even having to look. I had a feeling it would be a strong competition, but her lower calorie choice couldn't hold a candle to my pork chops, though.

"Beautiful! I'll have three please!" The two of them giggled together like best friends.

Christmas music hummed in the background while the obnoxious tree and the makeshift fireplace sparkled. I couldn't wait to rewatch this live when I got home that night. I'd rewatched the first round, interested to see how it all looked on the screen. The stupid hats aside, it was a dope setup.

"Okay. Time is running out. How's it looking, chefs?" Rodrigo called out.

"I'm good." I replied. Serenity and Audrey both chimed in with a 'me too'

Once everything was plated, I finally relaxed my shoulders. There had been tension building in them while I was cooking. I wanted to make sure everything was perfect. If the judges didn't like these pork chops, I'd have to question whether or not they belonged in the kitchen. This meal could convert a vegetarian with ease.

"That's time!" I stepped away from my station with my hands up. One step closer to taking this prize money home with me. The judges positioned themselves in front of our stations, ready to try their samples of our dishes. Chef Flamsey looked especially interested in my entrée.

"Alright, Handsome," Rodrigo gestured to me with a dramatic flourish, "Tell us about your dish!"

"I have for you guys my famous Glazed Honey Balsamic Pork Chops with Garlic Parmesan Potatoes." I tried to keep my face neutral as they picked up their plates, but the look of pure satisfaction on all three of the judges' faces made it hard to control my smile.

"This is absolutely delicious. Tell me, what's your secret for tender pork chops?"

"Cook them low and slow." I replied with a wink. In my peripheral, I could see Audrey roll her eyes and shake her head. If Jai was watching the Live, he was probably doing the same. The judges moved to her station next, studying her presentation with interest. That same confidence I saw in the first round clicked on as soon as they were in front of her table. She squared her shoulders, straightened her posture, and smiled brightly.

While she spoke, I found myself marveling at her beauty. Her flawless skin was smooth like chocolate and her curves, well-earned from countless nights in the gym, were on full display in her dark jeans and form fitting red sweater. My gaze drifted to her lips while she talked, zeroing in on the way they moved around certain words.

"Wonderful! And Serenity, dear. Tell us about your dish!" I blinked, surprised. I'd missed everything Audrey had said and the judge's reactions to her food because I was so focused on her lips. I cleared my throat awkwardly, hoping no one had noticed me zoning out.

Glitter from my Santa hat had somehow gotten on my hands. A sigh escaped my lips. It was obvious my face was covered in this mess. I would be washing it off for the next few days. I glanced over at Audrey with a smile. Glitter was all her hair and the shoulders of her sweater. This wasn't the best choice of costume for this round. Hopefully, the judges wouldn't penalize us for having glitter particles in the food.

While the judges deliberated, my mind drifted back to Audrey. I didn't want to look at her out of fear of her being able to sense what I was thinking. I knew I had one shot to transform things between us and I didn't want to ruin what could be something great.

"Alright! The judges have chosen a winner. Gather 'round!" Rodrigo clapped his hands together to grab our attention. We stepped forward, standing shoulder to shoulder while we waited to hear their decision.

"So, everyone's dish was incredible this time around." Chef Gordon paused long enough to make eye contact with each of us. "But unfortunately, not everyone can win."

"The winner of this round is..."

"Montrell Davis!" Rodrigo interrupted, excited. "Congrats, Handsome! Let's see what you win!"

We all turned to see one of the camera crew roll in a cart with a beautiful set of Japanese Chef Knives. If those were the knives I'd been drooling over recently, they were made of Damascus steel and incredibly expensive.

"This is dope. Thank you!" My mind went blank at that moment. Although confident in my entrée, I still expected Audrey to win. I turned to Serenity, my heart sinking at the look on her face. "I'm sorry, Serenity."

"Sorry? For what? This is a competition! You won fair and square." She smiled, even though it seemed a bit forced. "Congrats to you! Give me a hug!" She threw her arms around my neck before I had time to react.

"Listen, Audrey is a beautiful girl inside and out. Do NOT

screw this up, you hear me?" She whispered in my ear.

I pulled back, surprised. "What are you talking about?"

"Don't tell me you're in denial, too? Despite knowing you both for a short time, it's clear how you look at one another. Honey, Stevie Wonder could see it." We both looked over at Audrey, who was talking excitedly with Rodrigo. "She's a great girl. And incredibly talented."

I kept my eyes on Audrey, watching as she threw her head back and laughed. A small trail of glitter flickering down to the floor from her hat.

"Yeah," I sighed, "She is."

Chapter Eleven
Audrey

"Congratulations." Montrell looked up at the sound of my voice. He was crouching in front of the sauces in the pantry when I found him. At the immediate close of the competition, Serenity had grabbed me by the arm and pulled me to the side, so I hadn't had the chance to speak to him. Until now.

He straightened to his full height and turned to me. "Are we still good for dinner tonight?" His tone conveyed an unexpected hopefulness. Part of me assumed he wasn't serious about it and, in my mind, had already decided to do something else.

"Sure. What did you have in mind?"

"Well," He gestured towards the shelves stocked with food, "I figured there wouldn't be a restaurant that can make what we like better than we can."

"My place or yours?" I heard myself asking. He paused, looking me over, before gathering a few more things from the shelf.

"Yours is cool. I want to take a look at that mixer they gave you in the last round." My mind drifted back to the journal, currently burning a hole in my bag. I resisted the urge to peek at the new entry I was positive was waiting for me. "Is that okay with you?"

I blinked, embarrassed that he noticed me staring. "I- yeah. That's fine. I'm not sleeping with you, though." I blurted and then clamped my mouth shut, mortified. Montrell tilted his head, stunned at my outburst.

"I didn't realize that was even an option." He laughed.

"It's not." I shot back, fighting my smile. Even though, looking up at his broad shoulders and his piercing eyes had me briefly reconsidering that declaration. He grabbed a few more items from the shelves while I watched, struggling to find something to say. Should I try for a conversation? Was I really about to bring him into my house?

"What are you planning to make?" I asked. Montrell studied the jar he held, his brows furrowing together as he read the ingredients.

"It's a surprise." He replied, not looking up from what he was doing. I chewed my lip. A twinge of excitement formed in the pit of my stomach. I usually did most, if not all of the cooking in my relationships. Their biggest effort would involve ordering takeout. Having a man who knew exactly what he was doing in the kitchen cook for me was new. The thought of comparing what he and I were doing to past relationships made me shudder. I was definitely letting this journal get to my head. He was only offering to make something to eat and here I was already linking us like we go together. It was embarrassing.

"Do you want to go together?" Montrell asked. I jumped, shocked that he had heard what I was thinking. Did he have magical powers like this stupid journal did?

I blinked, stunned. My heart pounded in my chest. "What did you say?"

"I asked if you wanted to ride to your place together?"

I huffed out a breath, now feeling silly for thinking he could read my mind. His proximity was making me feel jittery, something I hadn't experienced in a while. Normally, I couldn't wait to get away from him, but now it felt like he was drawing me in somehow.

"No, that's okay. I have my car here. Let me send you the address really quick." I pulled out my phone. After sending him the address once he called out his number, I grabbed my things from the backstage room and jumped in my car, praying the entire way home that I wasn't making a mistake.

By the time I reached my apartment, my nerves were in overdrive. Montrell pulled up beside me and hopped out of his vehicle, looking much calmer and more collected than I was feeling at that moment. I envied his ability to seem so unbothered outside of the kitchen. Nothing seemed to faze him.

I unlocked my front door, grateful that I had cleaned up and decorated for the holiday a few days prior. My Christmas tree sat in the corner of the living room, its white string lights twinkling.

The blue and gold ornaments sparkled each time they caught the light. It was simple, but beautiful. Montrell came in behind me and placed the bags on the table.

"This is a dope spot." His simple comment made me swell with pride. Before I could respond, Chili came barreling around the corner. I tensed, unsure of how Montrell felt about dogs. It completely escaped my mind to ask before we got here. Chili ran straight for him, jumped up, and placed both front paws on his chest. I reached out, prepared to apologize, but to my surprise, he grinned and scratched her behind the ears.

"And who is this?" He asked. Her tail thumped, tongue lolling out to the side.

"This is Chili."

"What's up Chili? I'm Montrell." She tilted her head, as if understanding him, and then barked excitedly. I kicked off my shoes as Montrell continued talking to my dog as if she was a human and could respond, while she stared up at him like the sun rose and set on him. It looked like I was watching my dog replace me as her favorite human in real time.

I wanted to be annoyed by her betrayal, but I couldn't help but smile. They seemed to be old friends, comfortable and familiar with each other. Chili had always been a social dog, but this was new for even her. I'd never seen her connect with someone so easily.

My phone rang, distracting me from the bonding session unfolding in front of me. It was Deja. I answered the phone while I sorted through the items Montrell had grabbed from the pantry. "Hey girl!"

"Hey! I watched this round live. Sorry you didn't win."

"That's fine."

"Rodrigo announced on his channel that the last round would be filmed in front of an audience, so I wanted to tell you. I wanted to invite a few of my connects to come view the show. It could be good for you getting your name out there. Have you been posting like I told you?" I winced, feeling guilty even though she couldn't see me. I had been so wrapped up in the contest that I'd forgotten to stay consistent with posts.

Deja sighed in my ear. "I take your silence as a no."

"I'm sorry! It's so much to remember." Montrell shooed me out of the way and turned to wash his hands. I watched him for a moment, enjoying how at home he looked in my kitchen. This was his first time here, but he moved around as if he knew exactly where everything was. I stepped out of his way so I could keep talking.

"I figured. Don't worry. I've clipped both rounds up. We'll have enough material for a good number of reels.

"I'm not even sure what those words mean," I laughed. "But thank you. This wouldn't be possible without you."

"As long as you're aware of my ingenuity." She sniffed. "What are you doing, anyway? I'm about to come over."

"Um. Raincheck on that. I have a guest at the moment."

"Who?" Deja asked, skeptically.

"... Montrell." There was a moment of silence before Deja let out a high-pitched squeal and started pelting me with questions. None of which I really wanted to answer at this moment.

"Gotta go. Bye!" I hung up, even though I could still hear her talking as I pulled the phone away from my ear. I knew I'd be receiving a barrage of texts any minute, demanding to know what was going on. She might even rope the rest of the girls into the conversation if I didn't respond fast enough. I'd have to deal with all of that later. At this moment, my focus was solely on one person. The man who was standing in my kitchen with his sleeves rolled up to his elbows, looking like a model in a chef magazine spread. My throat tightened.

"Need any help?"

"Can you handle being in the kitchen with me?" He asked, his eyes still fixed on the vegetables he was chopping. I know he meant it as a joke, but my mind flashed back to the last time we cooked together. The final project in school that he ruined and then made me take the fall on.

"You know what? Never-mind." I replied sharply. His head snapped up, surprised at the change in tone. I glared at him. I thought I was past it, but everything from that night flooded back. He dumped the vegetables into the wok and turned the stove on low. The gentle sizzling of the veggies over the heat briefly distracted me.

"I was just kidding, Audrey. My bad."

"No, that's not it. I just-" I began. He put down the knife he was holding and waited for me to finish. Standing there with his eyes on me, focused so intently on whatever I had to say, made me clam up. I wanted to fuss at him, but I couldn't find the words to do it. The silence continued to stretch on; until his expression softened.

"I owe you an explanation. About that night." He said solemnly, nodding as if he understood what I was struggling to say.

"You don't owe me anything." I snapped, folding my arms.

"I do." I looked away as he came around the counter to stand in front of me. "Not that it's any excuse. That was a horrible day for me, and I've regretted it ever since. I don't know if Elodie ever told you, but my brother and I were in foster care for a while."

I nodded. She had mentioned it when they'd first started talking last year, around this time. Montrell and his brother, Mekhi, were in foster care until their foster parents adopted them and welcomed them into their family. From what Elodie had told me, Mekhi's decision to adopt his foster child, Kellan, stemmed from that experience.

"Our parents adopted us, and Mekhi had no problem accepting that it was our new reality. I struggled a bit more with it. For a while, our birth mother kept coming around every so often. Especially when she had gotten clean." He swallowed and looked away. I wanted to hug him, but I stayed where I was.

"That day before we were supposed to cook for the panel, she'd convinced me to meet her for breakfast. Mekhi had advised me not to. He'd cut ties with her long before then, but I had a harder time letting go. Anyway, the money I had given her to get herself a place was used to get high again." Montrell shook his head, his eyes glassy. "My anger clouded my judgment while we were cooking, and when the dish was ruined, I tried to explain what happened to the professor, but he misunderstood me. I'm sorry. It's not an excuse. I should have spoken up. I was just so embarrassed for allowing myself to fall for her game again that I couldn't think about anything else."

"He tried to convince me to sleep with him." I whispered. It was the first time I'd said it out loud.

I watched as Montrell stiffened, his expression hardening. "He did what?"

"For my grade. He said if I slept with him then he would pass me."

"Is that why you were crying when you came out of his office? Why didn't you tell me? I would have beat his-"

"I didn't need you to save me." I interrupted, folding my arms across my chest.

"I know you don't need it, Audrey. You can handle yourself, but that doesn't change me wanting to beat his face in after hearing you tell me he tried to take advantage of you." The anger in his voice surprised me.

"He also told me that you said it was my fault."

"No. That's not what I said at all. I said it was a complicated recipe, and I should have been more vocal about changing it." Montrell shook his head. "All this time. If I'd have known...I could have fixed it."

"It was messed up that you let me drown like that." I wanted to be mad, but hearing his explanation and seeing the remorse on his face crumbled the wall I had started to build around my heart.

"You're right. I'm so sorry for letting you down, but I can promise it'll never happen again." I diverted my eyes, but he tilted my chin, so I was forced to look at him. I couldn't help but see the sincerity in his expression. We stood there, staring at each other for a moment, his gaze dipping to my mouth and returning to my eyes. I caught myself looking at his lips, wondering what they would taste like, wondering if they were as soft as they looked.

"Your vegetables are burning." I whispered. He blinked, too locked into the moment to realize what I was saying.

"Huh?" He asked and then his eyes grew wide. "Oh! The vegetables!" I stifled a laugh as he ripped away from me and rushed over to the stove. They weren't completely burnt, just a little brown around the edges. While he cooked, I gave myself a chance to mull over what he had just shared with me. Was it enough to completely forgive that night?

"Come taste this," Montrell's voice snapped me out of my thoughts. He held out a fork with some of the stir fry he had just made on it. "Let me know if it needs anything."

I stood from my seat and opened my mouth. He guided the fork to my mouth, using his other hand to catch anything that fell. When I tasted the stir fry, my eyes rolled to the back of my head. Despite its simplicity, the dish he made was incredibly flavorful.

"It's perfect." I groaned.

"Of course." He grinned, taking a bite for himself. "Nothing less than perfection here."

After fixing our plates, we headed into my living room to get comfortable. Chili trailed behind us, hoping to catch any food we dropped. I noticed how easily he fit in around here, acting like he had been here all along. He settled in beside me and took a bite of his food.

"Do you want to watch the live? It's probably available by now."

I asked, turning on the television.

"That's fine." I pulled up the live that had been uploaded to YouTube and let it play. Rodrigo bounced around the screen, darting from one station to the next, keeping the viewers entertained. I found my gaze drifting to Montrell as he prepared the dish that won the round. He moved with such confidence, seasoning and searing the meat before placing it in the oven. Then, to my surprise, he turned toward my station and began watching me. The camera man zoomed in on his face while he watched me cook. I felt him stiffen beside me as we both watched him staring with fascination at me while I had been too focused on cooking to notice.

"Why are you watching me so hard?" I asked, laughing quietly. A beat of silence passed before he spoke, as if he struggled to find the words. I expected him to make a joke or brush off the question, but he turned to me, his eyes full of an intensity I wasn't prepared for.

"I can't help it." He admitted.

"What do you mean?"

"Think about it. Why am I always commenting on your social media? Why did I put my restaurant so close to yours? Why am I close by literally every time you look up?" He waited for me to respond, but I couldn't. The words got lodged in my throat. Instead, I focused on chewing my food thoroughly and swallowing it.

"It means that...you're stalking me." I replied feebly, trying to stave off the heat that was rising through my entire body, making it difficult to take in a deep breath.

"It means that for some reason, I'm drawn to you." I kept eating and staring at the screen, not knowing what to really say. The journal warned me we would get closer, but even knowing that, I wasn't prepared for it to happen. I hadn't expected that being so close to him would make my insides feel like mush. The desire to kiss him surprised me.

"Look at me," He whispered, setting his plate down on the coffee table in front of us. "Audrey."

Hearing my name on his lips was enough to snap me out of the trance. I put my plate down next to his and turned to him, fully aware of what would happen next, and desperately wanting it to happen. When our eyes locked, something unfurled inside of me.

"Kiss me." I demanded.

Without hesitation, he closed the distance between us and pressed his lips against mine. He followed my lead, matching my intensity with a burning fire of his own. As the kiss deepened, I shifted and threw my leg over his, so I was sitting in his lap. He cupped my butt in his massive hands and pulled me closer.

I let out a small whimper, desperate for more, but not wanting to go too far. He squeezed me a little tighter, causing another involuntary noise to leave my lips. The sound only made him kiss me harder as the tension that had been building between us bubbled over into passion.

He pulled away to look at me, both of us breathing hard and ragged. "You do not know how long I've wanted to do that."

"Hang on a second." I got off his lap and headed to my room, trying not to make a scene, but testing a theory for the journal. Sure enough, when I opened my bedroom door, the pages of the journal were flipping wildly until it landed on the last page. Words appeared on the page as soon as I stepped in and closed the door behind me.

Dear Diary,

  It finally happened. After all the tension, the bickering, the constant back-and-forth between Montrell and Audrey — they kissed. It felt like everything had been building to this moment without anyone realizing it. One second, they were watching television, finally getting along, and the next, the space between them just... disappeared.
  The quiet pause, their gaze spoke volumes, conveying unspoken emotions. And then Montrell leaned in, and Audrey didn't pull away. The moment was quiet and inevitable, not rushed or dramatic, as if all their walls had fallen at once.
  They finally embraced the emotions they had suppressed for so long.

Chapter Twelve
Montrell

Audrey returned to the room, clearly distressed and searching as if she was looking for someone else. She'd unexpectedly ripped herself away from me and went running into the bedroom as soon as things heated between us. It didn't seem like she was expecting me to follow. Instead, I'd been sitting there regaining control over my lower half while I waited. She sat down next to me with an apologetic grin on her face.

"This is moving a little fast for me." She winced, as if expecting me to get angry. Her words were like a splash of cold water on my entire body, snatching me out of the moment completely. I nodded, unsure of what else to say, and tried my best to readjust without making it too obvious. I needed something else to focus on until the rest of me could get the message. Nothing was going to happen between us, at least not tonight. I had to be okay with that. I reached for the food I had discarded when things had heated between us and took a bite. The chill didn't stop me from eating, unwilling to make her uncomfortable by halting the meal. Even though I desperately wanted to cup her face in my hands and kiss her until her lips were swollen.

"I'm sorry." I blurted, after a moment of tense silence had passed. "I want to avoid making you feel any kind of way. I didn't mean to-"

She shook her head, "No! Don't get me wrong, I want this. It's just... everything is moving so fast. It's making my head spin. Plus, we've hated each other for so long."

"That's not true. You've hated me. Sure, that part was obvious," I clarified, "But I've never hated you. Your refusal to let me explain myself frustrated me. But I never hated you. I don't think it's even possible to hate you." She stared at me, stunned by my admission.

"Why didn't you ever say anything?" She asked quietly.

"When? Between arguing every time we were within five feet of each other? Or when we were competing in our restaurants? It seemed like you didn't have any interest in changing the dynamic between us. I didn't want to push."

"So, what changed now, then?"

I shrugged. "I guess I just tired of us being enemies."

Her gaze quickly shifted over my shoulder toward her bedroom before landing back on me. I wanted to question why she had started acting shifty, but I didn't push. If there was something going on, she would tell me when she was ready. Hopefully.

"Is the Grinch really your favorite Christmas movie?" She asked, her mouth twitching like she was hiding a smile.

"Not really. It's Kellan's favorite. It was the first thing I could think of with Rodrigo staring at me so hard." We both laughed. Rodrigo was intense with his sparkles and his stiff hair full of hairspray. It was impossible to know if he was just acting for the cameras or if his true self was as flashy and glamorous.

"You should have just said This Christmas. Or Jingle Jangle."

"I haven't seen either of those, actually." Her mouth fell open as if I had just said something wild. I laughed, "Is that crazy?"

"Absolutely! We have to remedy this immediately." She grabbed the remote off the coffee table and opened her Netflix app. I watched as she tucked her feet under herself and settled further into the couch, like she was getting ready for a long night. "Settle in. You're not allowed to leave until you've seen at least one of them."

I did as I was told, sliding down into the couch and propping my feet up on the coffee table. I felt a bit tired after today's round, but I wouldn't dare admit that out loud for fear of this moment ending. It didn't matter how tired I was, I wouldn't trade this for anything else.

"Which one do you want to watch first?" She asked.

"You pick." I replied. To be honest, I didn't care what we watched. I couldn't promise that I'd pay attention through all of it, but I knew it made her happy, and that was something I didn't get to see often. It was one of the few times we were together that didn't begin with her berating me, and if I played my cards right, it wouldn't end that way, either.

"Jingle Jangle it is, then." She clicked on the movie and patted the couch beside her. Chili, who had been laying at my feet, hopped up beside Audrey and curled into her side. Observing them, I realized how much I longed for such shared moments with someone special. In past relationships, we'd never had chill moments like this where we were together, just enjoying each other's company. Emotional turmoil was always involved somehow. I'd find myself even more exhausted after seeing them than I had been when I'd first arrived. Being able to be in someone's presence and feel a sense of peace was new.

I focused my attention back on the movie, figuring I'd give it a shot since Mekhi had also raved about how unexpectedly entertaining the entire thing was. He'd mentioned forcing Elodie and Kellan to watch it with him at least three times already this year. He'd been trying to get me to look at it since it first came out. I hadn't been interested. Until now.

When the end credits rolled up on the screen, I blinked, shocked that I had sat up and watched this entire thing. I'd expected to zone out or fall asleep, but to my surprise, I ended up enjoying the movie. Audrey shifted, so she was facing me and smiled.

"What did you think?"

"It's not bad. The singing got a little ridiculous in some spots, but for a Christmas movie, it entertained me.

Her smile widened, taking over her entire face. It was contagious. I could feel myself smiling back at her, grinning from ear to ear like a kid. It's ridiculous what this girl is doing to me. I stood and stretched, trying not to let the yawn I felt building up come out.

"If you're tired, you can go home. I won't keep you," she said, studying my face. I guess the exhaustion was showing more than I realized. Even though my entire body was screaming at me to go home and get some rest, I wasn't ready for this night to end yet. Her mere presence was enough to satisfy me, even without anything physical.

"Not a chance." I replied. "We can watch This Christmas next. Do you have any popcorn? We could make some while we watch the next movie."

"I'll check and see." I watched as she went back into the kitchen. Chili took her absence as a chance to come crawling back to me. She slid forward on her belly, on the couch until her head was in my lap. I'd heard about Doodles being friendly dogs, but this was unexpected. It made me want a dog of my own. Maybe once Audrey and I officially start dating, we can get another dog to hang out with Chili while we're at work.

I'd surprised myself by imagining what a future would look like when we hadn't even made it through the night yet. It felt a little premature, to say the least, but I couldn't help it. Now that I had put my feelings out there, I couldn't swallow them back down. Even if I wanted to.

"Have you ever thought about another dog?" I followed her into the kitchen while she looked through her cabinets for popcorn.

"What's wrong with my current dog?" She asked, looking over

at Chili, who had trailed in behind the two of us, hoping for a snack. "She may be lazy, but that's not reason enough to get rid of her."

"No, I'm saying getting another dog. So, she has someone to talk to."

"Who's going to handle two dogs? Chili already requires most of my attention. You want me to add another one to the mix?" She laughed, opening a few of the cabinets.

"I'd help." She stopped searching for the popcorn and turned to look at me. I hoped my face looked as sincere as I felt. She silently studied my face, a mixture of emotions I couldn't read passing over hers.

"Take me slow, Montrell. Before you offer me a white picket fence and a happily ever after."

"My bad. I'm just saying." I laughed, "Consider it." Things fell silent between us while she popped a bag of popcorn for us to share during the next movie. I'd promised Jai I'd be in early to go over the possibility of a new menu, but I might have to push that meeting back.

"Where's your bathroom?" I asked.

"The guest bathroom is out of commission currently, so just use mine. Second door on the left." She replied, pointing over her shoulder as she reached for a bowl to put the popcorn in. I tried not to make a big deal out of her, giving me permission to go into her bedroom. It was like an opportunity to see a part of her I'd never seen before. I entered the room, not surprised to find an eclectic set up, not unlike her restaurant.

A queen-sized bed took up most of the wall in the middle of

the room, with a desk and an entertainment system big enough for her television. A large closet sat to my right with the door cracked open slightly. The room itself smelled faintly of vanilla and jasmine, remnants of the perfume she had been wearing today.

I stood in the doorway for a minute, taking in the layout in front of me. I could see myself in here, permanently. It was wild that we had barely established what we were, and I was already finding ways to make my presence a permanent fixture in her life. Before, thinking about the future only included me, myself, and I, but now, I found myself mentally shifting things around to make room for Audrey and Chili. I wanted the both of them with me, forever. I'm willing to do whatever it takes to make that happen. I shook my head, clearing my mind, and stepped forward. There was a book on her bed lying open. I glanced at it, tempted to pick it up, and then walked past. Snooping would not be a good look, no matter how curious I was.

Her bathroom smelled like Christmas evergreen and holly, and the decor matched her theme in the living room. I shook my head, stifling a laugh. Of course, she would decorate a bathroom that nobody would use but her, on the off chance that someone would somehow see it.

I finished up and then closed the bathroom door behind me. That book I had noticed on my way in lay on her bed, still untouched. Something about it drew my attention. I stared at it, trying to figure out what it was about it that made me so interested in it. She's not the first to keep a journal and she wouldn't be the last. Prying into her personal thoughts was not something I wanted to do, but I moved towards it, wanting to get a look at what was inside.

My feet ached to turn and head for the door, but my will was powerless against the pull of the journal. An invisible force propelled me forward, despite my desperate resistance. I stepped closer to the journal and reached out for it, my hands overriding the commands from my brain to step away and leave the room. I glanced nervously over my shoulder to make sure she wasn't coming. This felt like a seriously underhanded move. I could see some words written on the open page.

The handwriting was similar to something I'd seen on an old school typewriter. Upon closer inspection, it looked like there were a few entries in it. Maybe Audrey had been in the process of writing in her journal before she had left for the show this morning. Or maybe that's what she was in here doing when she ran away while we were kissing. She had been gone for a few minutes and I'd been so focused on making sure the blood flowed back into my extremities that I hadn't noticed.

I picked it up and flipped through it. To my surprise, each entry I saw was something about me. My name was in every single entry at least twice. The entire thing was about how we were meant to be together, and we were getting closer. It gave me a weird feeling. If she truly felt this way, why did she pretend to despise me for so long?

Why did she leave me out here thinking I had to prove myself to her? And why, now that we are seeing eye to eye and getting closer, is she pushing me away? The more I read, the more annoyed I became. The Audrey who wrote this and the Audrey I knew felt like two separate individuals. Nothing matched.

The journal entries documented our gym encounter and every interaction afterward. It felt like I was reading through a script of everything we had talked about since that moment. And yet, whenever I expressed an interest in moving things forward with her, she acted like this whole concept was new and foreign to her. When she had been in here writing about it all along. Part of me felt like maybe I should be happy about this, but the disconnect was too loud for me to ignore it. So hot and cold that it made my head spin.

"Hey, what's-" Audrey appeared in the doorway, a smile on her face that quickly faded when she saw what I was holding. "What are you doing?" She asked, her voice taking on an accusatory tone.

"What is this?" I demanded, holding it up for her to see. "You keep stalling on us moving forward in real life, but on paper, you keep talking about how we're meant to be?"

"It's not what it looks like..." she began, and then chewed on her bottom lip. "I didn't write any of it. It's a journal that Elodie gave me. She said it's what brought her and Mekhi together."

"How could a journal be responsible for that?" None of what she was saying made sense. It felt like she wasn't taking me seriously. What other reason could she have for inventing such a nonsensical excuse?

"It's magical." Her voice was feeble, as if even she didn't believe what she was saying. I stared at her, irritation burning like fire in the pit of my stomach.

"If you're not ready to talk about it, that's one thing, but don't lie to me."

"Why were you reading my journal, anyway? Let's discuss that!"
She shot back. I paused, unsure of what to say. I don't know why
I was reading her stuff. It's not even like me to go snooping like
this, but something pulled me in that direction. I can't deny that.

"Forget it. I'm not doing this with you. If you don't want to
be honest, then I'm gone." I grabbed my keys and my phone
and headed towards the door. As soon as I stepped out of the
threshold and closed the front door behind me, a wave of regret
washed over me. Maybe I was overreacting.

Chapter Thirteen
Montrell

It was Christmas Eve and finally the last round of this contest. Audrey and I were due to compete against each other for the prize money, but all I could think about was having her in my arms again. We stood on the set under the heavy lights and Christmas decorations. An entire audience full of our loved ones and random people Rodrigo managed to dredge up, sat watching to see what would happen.

When Jai entered me in this contest, I'd had no idea I would end up cooking against Audrey Bennett. Even more so, I'd had no idea that we would have ended up sharing a moment in her apartment. Things got weird after I saw that journal, but I can admit that I overreacted.

The idea that it brought her to me is actually comforting. I don't know if she would have ever given me the chance to explain myself had *Sleigh the Recipe* not put her on the path towards me. Now, here we were, on the final round of this competition, and all I could think about was making sure the distance that had been created between us would not continue. I wanted to be around her as much as possible. I needed to be around her.

Before all of this, I had been so adamant about not settling down because I didn't think love was in the cards for me. I'd scoffed at my brother meeting his girlfriend and being willing to readjust his life completely so their relationship would make sense. I never believed I would meet anyone that'd have me ready to hang up my Toque if it meant we would have a fighting chance. Little had I known, the one person who would have me willing to do that, had been two doors down all along. After our night together, I couldn't stop thinking about the future and what it meant for the two of us. As long as we were together, I'd figure out the rest.

"Alright my beauties, we are here. The last hoorah. Final round of *Sleigh the Recipe*!" Rodrigo began, clapping his hands together in mock sadness. Dramatic music played in the background. I shook my head, trying to conceal my smile. I would miss him and his shenanigans when this was all said and done. "Tell us, how do you feel?"

"Feels great to be here." I replied, shrugging. The bells on the hat they forced me to wear, jingling under my movement. I wasn't able to see myself, but I knew I looked ridiculous in this ugly Christmas sweater and obnoxious headwear.

"I'm so excited to get started!" Audrey chimed in, smiling brightly at the camera. The silly Christmas attire did nothing to dampen her beauty.

"Love to hear it. But first, tell us what you'll do with the prize money when you win those ten thousand dollars!"

"I plan to put it towards some renovations at The Hungry Hippo." Jai had already started sending me lists of things that needed updating, as if I'd won the prize money. I could see him in the audience out of the corner of my eye, clapping wildly at my statement. I ignored him as best as I could. Rodrigo nodded at my answer and gestured towards Audrey, who had been nervously readjusting her hat while I talked.

"And you, doll?" Rodrigo prompted.

"Me? Oh!" her cheeks flushed, "To be fully transparent, Audrey's Kitchen hasn't been doing too great lately. So, I'm hoping to put the money towards promotions and advertising to bring in more business. Hoping to get my name and my skill out there. This is just the first stop!"

Hearing her admit that her restaurant was struggling a bit, made my heart break. After being in this competition with her and hearing her talk about her dad being the inspiration for Audrey's Kitchen, I knew how much the place meant to her and how much it would crush her to lose it. I glanced over at Jai, who widened his eyes subtly as a way to tell me not to do whatever it was that I was thinking. After knowing me for so long, he knew when I was plotting something, sometimes even before I started. He could see it all over my face even from where he sat.

"Well, good luck to you both! This round is called Sweet Tidings. It is up to you to make a delicious Christmas treat that exemplifies the spirit of the holiday and wows the judges. Are we ready?"

Audrey and I both nodded. With his usual dramatics and flair, Rodrigo waved his arms wildly, signaling for us to go ahead and begin. "Go! Go! Go!"

We both took off towards the pantry for the last time. I had to admit that I would miss this when it was over. I had come to look forward to cooking under pressure. It gave me a chance to really test my skills. Christmas music played softly in the background. It sounded like a Pentatonix rendition of Jingle Bells. Worse than Mariah Carey, that group always popped up around Christmas ready to redo the songs we knew and loved with their own beatboxing and high-pitched singing. I could hear the audience chattering amongst themselves, full of excitement at watching the contest unfold. I'd decided to make Salted Caramel S'mores, one of my favorite desserts to whip out on a cheat day during the colder months.

I caught Audrey's eye on the way out of the pantry; she gave me a small smile before heading to her station to begin her dessert. There was a hint of sadness and something else that I couldn't place in her expression. I wanted to halt the entire competition right there so I could find out what was wrong, but instead, I scanned the shelves for the items I would need. As I looked, my mind drifted back to her admission before we got started. Her spot was losing business probably because there was a competing restaurant not even two doors down that was stealing some of the customers. In my desperation to be close to her, to somehow be in her orbit, however I could manage it, I had actually hurt her business. It finally clicked. My actions, however well-intentioned, did more harm than good. I needed to make it up to her and there was only one way to do that. It was then, in that moment, that I knew what I had to do. I could only hope Jai would forgive me.

I grabbed the cinnamon, unsalted butter, kosher salt, some molasses and whole wheat pastry flour to bring back with me to my station. It was a simple enough recipe, and it put me finishing right at the end of the round, so there wouldn't be much time left to overthink what I was about to do. The room was quiet, aside from the music playing in the background. Everyone watched with bated breath as we worked silently at our stations. My mind felt like it was whirling a mile a minute, each thought tumbling over the other one as my hands moved on autopilot.

I made the dough for the graham crackers and cut them into squares. Once finished, I placed them on a cookie sheet and stuck them in the oven so they could bake for about twenty minutes. The trick to making this treat so delicious was making each ingredient. No store-bought crackers would be allowed in this dessert, even though they came in handy if pressed for time and not trying to impress a panel of judges. While the crackers baked, I headed back to the pantry to get the semi-sweet chocolate squares, marshmallows, and some caramel sauce I had spotted the week before when I was sifting through the stocked shelves.

"What are you making, Montrell?" Rodrigo asked, coming to peek over the counter at my station. I noticed that he didn't have a pet name for me this time.

"I'm making Salted Caramel S'mores." I replied, placing my items on the counter space.

"That sounds delicious! What inspired this choice?"

"It's a fun dessert that I break out around the colder months of the year. Nothing like a good S'more to really kick off the holiday season." I could hear the whispers from the crowd. Audrey's friend Deja was front and center watching her friend bake and filming on her own phone, most likely for videos to post later. Audrey had told me her friend Deja was a genius when it came to branding and marketing, always thinking two steps ahead. Jai, on the other hand, was preoccupied with staring at the woman sitting next to Deja. Even from all the way on the other side of the room, I could tell he was drooling over her like a lovesick puppy.

I shook my head. If he was already that far gone, he probably wouldn't even notice what was happening over here. My watch buzzed on my wrist to signify that the crackers were done in the oven, but I didn't get them out right away. I let them sit in the oven and turned my attention to Audrey just in time to see Rodrigo slide over to her station.

"Tell us what you're making, Audrey."

"Chocolate-Chip-Pecan Cookie bars." She replied proudly. "My dad and I used to make these cookie bars every Christmas to leave out for Santa. I always wanted to make sure he had another sweet treat to choose from since he was probably tired of cookies." The image of a child version of Audrey being concerned about Santa getting sick of cookies made me shake my head. I couldn't believe how far gone I was. I had just laughed at Jai, when I was no better.

"Alright. That's time!" Chef Flamsey called a few moments later. My S'mores were plated and ready to go. The smell of the caramel mixed with the chocolate from both of our dishes was enough to make me want to reach out and snag a bite. We were instructed this time to make enough for our guests as well as the judges. I had three special plates for the judges that I set to the side.

Chef Flamsey passed out the plates to the other two judges. My heart jumped in my throat, as they bit into them, knowing exactly this reaction I would receive. Flamsey coughed and made a face. Chef Bordon spit out the small bite he had taken.

"This is a nice concept, but it's incredibly salty." Chef Gemerald put his plate down and slid it as far away as he could get it. I nodded, making sure to look as sad as I could manage.

"That's so unfortunate." Rodrigo said sadly, "You must have overdone it on the salted part of the salted caramel."

I shrugged, making sure to avoid eye contact with Audrey for fear that she would catch on. "Mistakes happen. What can you do?"

The judges moved down to her station. Out of the corner of my eye, I could see her staring at me, but she said nothing, and I kept my gaze straight ahead. I didn't want to give myself away, not until the decision was already made. Audrey handed each Chef a plate with one of the cookie bars and beamed excitedly.

"Oh wow. This is delicious. The cookie has the right amount of gooey and firmness to it." Her smile widened and I couldn't help but grin myself.

"Time for the judges to deliberate!" Rodrigo clapped. All four of them stepped off to the side to discuss, leaving Audrey and I to stand there with each other and wait. She stared at me, studying my expression. I tried my hardest to meet her gaze with a blank look, but she saw right through me.

"You purposely botched your dessert, didn't you?" She demanded, narrowing her eyes. Before I could respond, Rodrigo stepped out of the group and turned to us.

"It is a unanimous decision!" He announced, his glittery red tuxedo sparkling under the many lights. The judges lined up in front of us, all of them silently staring straight ahead. I had to give Rodrigo his credit, this entire production has been quite an experience. His flair for the dramatics made everything fit together. Even the tackiest of elements, like these stupid Christmas sweaters they forced us to put on before we began filming, all came together to make this a production worth remembering.

"The winner of *Sleigh the Recipe* and the ten-thousand-dollar grand prize, is..."

A drumroll played from somewhere and a hush fell over the audience. If someone chose this moment to drop a pen, everyone would have been able to hear it. I held my breath, hoping my efforts paid off.

"Audrey Bennett!" At the sound of her name, Audrey's mouth fell open in shock. Happy tears filled her eyes and spilled down her cheeks. A loud shriek from the audience drew my attention away from her reaction. All four of her friends came rushing the stage, squealing and congratulating their friend.

I spotted Jai off to the side, observing the celebration. When our eyes connected, he approached me. "You've made those S'mores so many times you have the recipe down to a science. There's no way you messed up. You rigged it." He said simply, daring me to challenge him. There was no anger or malice in his voice, just a hint of resigned acceptance.

"I owed it to her." I replied.

Whether or not he agreed, I knew I'd done the right thing. We didn't need the money as badly as she did. If we revisited the budget and moved some things around, we could absolutely find the money for the renovations. She had a dream she was fighting for and deserved to see it through.

"Hey! Better luck next time, friend." Rodrigo said, coming up behind me.

"Yeah. I'm cool with it. She deserves it." I smiled. He studied me for a moment, narrowing his eyes slightly.

"You two make a beautiful couple."

"Oh no, we're not-" I began and then stopped. Truth be told, I had no idea what we were. I knew what I wanted us to be though, if she would have me. Audrey's friends had finally stopped jumping up and down excitedly. My brother Mekhi was there with his girlfriend Elodie and adopted son Kellan, talking with Audrey's friends. I remember meeting most of them last year at Mekhi's school musical. While I turned back to my station, attempting to clean up the leftovers from the judges' plates, I felt a hand on my shoulder. I glanced over my shoulder, expecting to see my brother and coming face to face with Audrey instead.

"Did you let me win?" She demanded, folding her arms across her chest.

"Of course not." I replied quickly.

"Montrell..." there was a warning in her tone. She already knew the answer but wanted to hear it from me.

"Look, you deserved this more than I did. I heard what you said about needing to save your restaurant. The Hungry Hippo is good. I've got everything I want aside from one thing."

"And what is that?"

"You." I could tell my answer caught her off guard. She glanced around to see if anyone had heard me, but everyone else was preoccupied with eating the leftover treats and talking amongst themselves. "I don't care about this contest, I never did. All I care about is you."

"I'm not sure what to say." She chewed on her bottom lip. I pressed my hands into the counter to keep myself from reaching out to touch her. If I had my way, I'd scoop her up in my arms right now and kiss her, but we were standing in a room full of people.

"Say you'll give me a shot." I gave in to the urge to be close to her and stepped around the counter. She didn't pull away. Instead, she tilted her chin, so she was staring up at me, her beautiful lips only inches away from mine.

"I guess..." She turned her head, trying to hide her smile. I leaned in and kissed her, not caring who was paying attention.

Chapter Fourteen
Audrey

"Congratulations, boss lady! I knew you would win!" Anika squealed into my ear. It was Christmas morning the next day, and I had barely opened my eyes before my phone started going off with congratulation texts and phone calls. I'd turned my phone on silent in the middle of the night because the constant notification noise kept waking me up. News of the competition had spread and a few of the clips from each of the rounds had gone viral.

Serenity, who had become a fast friend since this contest started, already sent me a few that featured both of us creating our dishes. I was grateful that I didn't look as nervous as I'd felt on video. I was moving throughout my station with a confidence that commanded attention. It was my first time watching myself cook and I was surprised to see how in my element I looked. It felt odd being filmed while doing something that felt like second nature. I no longer had to really think about what I was doing, as soon as I decided what I would make, I let my instincts take over. They haven't steered me wrong yet.

She'd also sent me clips from the first round when Dot had humiliated herself in front of everyone after presenting a dish that was completely raw. Videos of her had also gone viral, with some of the comments dragging her and her lack of sportsmanship for filth. Her dramatic outburst had become a meme on the social media platforms, with people using the short clip to express when things hadn't gone their way. Part of me felt bad for her, having a moment that had to be embarrassing immortalized on the internet for hundreds and even thousands of people to witness. People love to see a disaster unfold, especially when that disaster had nothing to do with them.

"Thank you! Why are you calling me so early, though?" I cracked open an eye to look at the clock. "It's only six thirty." My entire body was still sore from the contest. I'd been holding my stress in my shoulders.

"Oh, right! About that. Your page has been blowing up since the contest started. People have been wanting to know when you'd be back at Audrey's Kitchen. Not sure what to tell them."

My eyes popped open, and I sat straight up in bed, Chili lifted her head to look at me, surprised by my sudden movements. I'd been completely ignoring my social media lately, choosing instead to let Deja take over the entire thing. A perk of having a marketing genius as my best friend. It gave me one less thing to obsess over while I had been preparing for the contest. I pulled the phone away from my ear and logged into the Facebook page. There were hundreds of new followers and tons of interactions on videos I hadn't even seen. Deja had told me she was clipping shots from the live and reposting them on my page, but I'd had no idea she was out here moving like this. I scrolled, eyes wide and mouth open in shock, skimming over some of the comments.

"Wow. I-" I breathed, suddenly feeling emotional. "I had no idea."

"Audrey's Kitchen is really about to be on the map, family. Uncle would be proud." At the mention of my late father, the emotions I'd been hit with spilled over. I'd been so scared this contest wouldn't work. I was so worried that I would participate in this contest, give it my absolute all and still end up a disappointment, but I should have known Deja would work magic. She saw something in Audrey's Kitchen that even I hadn't noticed was there.

After a moment of silence, Anika giggled softly, realizing that I had most likely gotten lost in my thoughts. "Like I said, I'm proud of you. But no, seriously though, are we opening today or nah? I've got a friend that I told I would go see before I got sucked into family gatherings."

I laughed at my cousin and wiped the tears from my eyes. Now wasn't the time to be emotional. "Today you guys deserve to enjoy your holiday. Tell them we will be back open tomorrow. Merry Christmas!" After we hung up, I let out an excited squeal.

"Everything okay?" A shirtless Montrell entered the bedroom and flopped down beside me. I had almost forgotten that he was here. I filled him in on everything while he scratched Chili behind the ears. He pulled out his own phone and scrolled through some of the comments, impressed. "This is dope. You deserve every ounce of this attention and more."

I felt overwhelmed with everything that was going on all at once. I won a contest; my restaurant is gaining popularity, and I was in a whole new relationship with the one guy I never thought I'd be with. If you'd told me when Deja first brought the competition to my attention, that it would lead me down the path that ended up here, with Montrell Davis in my bed, I'd have said you'd lost your mind.

"The Hungry Hippo has gotten a few extra customers since the competition. I think they're more interested in seeing our relationship though."

"They saw you staring at me the whole time." I replied. He shook his head and laughed.

Deja had told me that our budding relationship gained almost as much popularity as our food had. Some of the viewers tuned in solely to see whether or not we had moved forward with each other yet. The idea that so many people were out there, watching and rooting for us was oddly comforting and scary at the same time.

"Let me make you a congratulatory breakfast before I go. My French toast is immaculate. My brother might tell you that he taught me how to make it, but he stole the recipe from me. Don't let him fool you." Montrell reached for his shirt and tossed it over his shoulder, his well-earned muscles rippling under his skin as he moved. We had spent the night together after his declaration and I desperately wanted to spend the day laying around in bed with him. However, he'd told me his mother would have his head if he didn't spend the Christmas holiday with them, and I'd already promised my mom that I would stop by her place today to help cook.

"Can I help?" I asked.

"Not if you want us to actually have something edible." He grinned. I thumped him in the back and laughed. Even with us trying out this relationship, he never missed the opportunity to make a joke about my cooking. "You may have won the competition, Audrey Bennett, but we both know who the better chef is."

"In your dreams."

"Do you want to watch a movie while you cook?" I asked.

"Only if it's not Christmas related. I'm burnt out on the holiday after being forced to wear so many stupid hats."

"Elodie is probably going to make you wear one when you go to your parents' house today. If I know my girl, she has them all in matching holiday outfits." I laughed. He made a face and shuddered dramatically.

"Not doing that. I will not be participating. Only there to fill my duties as a son since I agreed to help out with dinner. Nothing more or less."

"Come on! Where's your Christmas cheer?"

He made a face, "I have none."

"Oh, aren't you a mean one, Mr. Chef?" I giggled at my own terrible Christmas pun as he shot me a withering glare and sighed. If I was honest, I was a little burnt on the holiday myself. The competition had taken quite a bit out of me. I was looking forward to coming back home and hanging out with my dog and my book for the night. I still had four more chapters to finish before the next Novel-Tea meeting. Didn't feel like hearing Elodie fuss me out again for not finishing the book in time. She cut us no slack, even during the holiday season.

I followed him into the kitchen with Chili trailing lazily behind us. The Christmas tree sparkled from where I'd left the lights on all night. Presents for my family and for my friends sat under the tree waiting to be unwrapped. My girls and I had decided against getting gifts for each other this year, but Elodie broke that promise at the last book club meeting. After that day, I'd gone out and gotten them each a little something, just to remind them of how much I loved them and appreciated their friendship.

I stopped in my tracks and stared at the tree. Something looked off and I couldn't quite figure out why. Montrell kept moving, not realizing that I had stopped walking behind him. It took me a moment to spot what was different. There was a small box I didn't recognize, sitting under the tree in beautiful sparkly green and blue paper. "What is that?"

"Open it and see." Montrell didn't turn to look at where I was pointing, just made a show of grabbing bowls and ingredients from the fridge as if this was his place and not mine. He moved through my kitchen as if it wasn't just the second time he'd been in here. I reached for the box, my hands trembling with anticipation. I had no idea what he'd gotten me for Christmas, and I felt guilty because I hadn't had the opportunity to give him anything. I gingerly pulled at the piece of tape holding the paper shut and ripped open the rest. Inside was a delicate gold chain with a whisk on the end of it.

"This is beautiful, thank you!" I exclaimed, taking it out of the box.

"I'm glad you like it." He fixed the clasp around my neck
and planted a quick kiss on my exposed shoulder. I turned and
wrapped my arms around his neck, pulling him closer to me.
He wrapped his arms around my waist. Things felt so natural
between us it was hard to believe that this was all still so new.

"I don't have anything for you, though."

"You are my Christmas gift."

"God, you're so corny." I pretended to gag, but not so secretly
loving every moment of it. I could stay in his arms forever, letting
the time pass us both by. If I didn't have a restaurant to run, I
would probably be spending as much time with him as I could.

"Get used to it, Bennet. You'll be hearing it from now on.
Whether you like it or not." I watched as he effortlessly made
breakfast for the two of us, contemplating the promise behind
his words. There was a permanence to that simple phrase that
settled in my heart. Whether I like it or not, and at this moment, I
definitely did.

My gaze drifted to the journal sitting on my kitchen table. I'd
taken it out of its usual place last night to let Montrell get a good
look through it. I could tell he didn't totally believe the concept
of the journal, but he was willing to humor me. I think Mekhi
had talked to him about it as well, so he'd already had some
knowledge of what was happening.

He followed my gaze, "Are there any new entries?"

Last night I hadn't bothered to check after coming home from
the competition. Now, the journal sat there taunting me, tempting
me to open it and check without making a sound. Even though

I'd seen it happen a few times now, the phenomenon still made me uneasy. I always felt the need to approach it with caution, as if something were going to jump out and grab me if I moved too quickly around it.

I held it as far away from my body as I could, just in case it decided to add 'explode' to the list of things it could do and flipped to the last page I remembered reading. Sure enough, there was an unfamiliar entry on the last page. Montrell watched me, his shoulders tense. I could tell he wasn't sure what to expect and honestly, neither was I. Elodie would always laugh at me whenever I expressed nervousness around the journal. She and her grandmother were used to it by now, but it was still scary for me. Every time it worked, I kept waiting for a ghost or something creepy to jump out.

"Yeah, there is a new entry in here."

"Okay. Don't keep me in suspense. What does it say? Are we due to win the lottery soon? Should I go play some numbers?"

"It's not that kind of journal." I replied, rolling my eyes at him.

"You say that as if it's normal to have a book that writes in itself." With a sigh, I began to read what the entry said out loud. Montrell continued to cook as he listened, the smell of bacon and eggs wafted through the house, making my stomach grumble.

Dear Diary,

   Montrell and Audrey finally realized it — they belong together. After years of tension, misunderstandings, and hiding

behind their arguments, they both just
stopped pretending and let things unfold
as they should. It wasn't a grand moment
or some dramatic confession. They were
just moving through the competition that
was destined to bring them together, and
suddenly, everything clicked.

Montrell admitted, almost shyly, how
much she meant to him, and for once, Audrey
didn't throw up her usual defenses. She
looked at him and said, "I think I've always
known." It was quiet, simple, and honest,
like they were finally letting themselves see
what had been there all along.

They need each other — always have, and
now that they're finally ready to embrace it,
the work here is done.

Chapter Fifteen

Audrey
Two Years Later

"Woman! You do this every single time!" Montrell huffed, irritated. We stood in my kitchen, moments before our friends were due to show up for Thanksgiving dinner, with absolutely no food prepared. As much as I didn't want to admit that I was ill-prepared, I absolutely was. I glanced around the kitchen, ignoring the stress building in my shoulders, as I concocted a plan.

Montrell had been bugging me since Tuesday to figure out a menu and start prepping to cook, but I kept procrastinating, determined to nail a recipe for my steadily growing Tik Tok channel before I directed my attention to Thanksgiving. Unfortunately, nailing the recipe had taken a lot longer than I thought. Prepping and filming for the video had spilled over into my Thanksgiving dinner prep time.

I regretted volunteering to take on the responsibility of dinner, but at the time I hadn't expected my new channel to get so much attention. I thought I would be making a few videos here and there, but no one informed me just how much work goes into curating creative videos. Trying to find new ways to showcase my recipes felt like a whole extra full-time job that I wasn't immediately getting paid for.

"Instead of fussing at me," I threw open the cabinets looking through my supplies and random ingredients hoping an idea would jump out at me, "Help me come up with something to feed everyone! They'll be here soon."

He folded his arms, not budging from his spot, "What's in it for me?"

"I'll make it worth your while." I promised, wiggling my eyebrows obnoxiously.

Montrell glared at me before his face softened, "You're lucky you're so damn cute. Makes it easy to forget how much stuff like this annoys me."

"It's part of my charm. Now, help me!" I glanced at the clock while I pulled out a bowl and some mixing spoons from my cabinet. We had maybe forty-five minutes before they would start showing up, and while my friends had become accustomed to my split focus, I knew it bothered Montrell having to come up with things on the fly. He sighed and turned to the sink to wash his hands, grumbling something about me never listening to him. Chili pawed at his thigh, causing him to glance down at her. She tilted her head, letting her ears flop to the side in a comical expression she often did when she was trying to understand what we were saying.

"You see what I have to go through, Chili?" He shook his head. Chili barked happily, tail wagging as if to agree with Montrell. She constantly hung on his every word, from the moment he met her until now. I was chopped liver in my own home. My own dog turned against me. After I was the one to feed and walk her and raise her as if she were a child birthed from my loins. The betrayal is real.

"You traitor!" Both of them turned to look at me, head tilting to the side in similar gestures, and I couldn't help but laugh at the sight. Chili had fallen head over heels with Montrell the night she met him, but judging from the way he would greet her before he even greeted me most days, the feeling was mutual.

While we hurried to create something edible for our guests coming over, I filled Montrell in on how my Tik Tok channel had been going. After the competition two years ago, my business had been steadily growing. Putting my name out there like Deja had encouraged me to do, had done nothing but bring in business. I ended up taking Serenity on as an extra chef on days when I was unable to work. After the contest, even though she didn't win, she was able to dislodge herself from her family's business and launch her own career. I had been more than happy to bring her on when she called me and asked me if I had any ideas. She has been a godsend for Audrey's Kitchen.

"Okay, so if we make enough of their favorite appetizers, they won't notice that this isn't the traditional Thanksgiving set up?" I asked hopefully, grabbing my muffin tin from out of the cabinet. I could do a few egg bites and maybe throw in some homemade mozzarella sticks for Kellan. They'd never know the difference. As long as they had something to eat, they'd be fine.

Montrell made a face at me. "You know Mekhi will be the first one to ask about a turkey. If by some miracle he doesn't then Monae will."

He was right. Those two ate me out of house and home every time I invited them over for dinner. It was like a competition between the two of them to see who could shovel in the most calories in one sitting. Mekhi usually won, but Monae would always give him a run for his money. Even Kellan, who was now a teenager and nursing a bottomless pit of an appetite of his own, couldn't keep up.

Chili sniffed around our feet, hoping one of us would accidentally drop a piece of food for her to nibble on. Finding nothing, she settled onto her bed by the door with a huff. I paused for a moment, truly seeing this moment for the first time. Two years ago, if you would have told me that I would be dating the one person I viewed as the bane of my very existence, I would laugh in your face. As a matter of fact, I did. Whenever the journal tried to push me in his direction, I fought against it with everything in me. When my friends tried to get me to see him in a different light, I refused. Little did I know, once I allowed things to happen, I found a level of happiness I didn't know existed.

That cooking competition, with the silly Christmas hats and the blaring lights and fake Christmas decorations, was the best thing that could have happened to me. It opened my eyes to someone who was right in front of me the entire time.

"Why are you staring at me?" Montrell asked, a smile on his lips.

I blinked, bringing myself back to the present.

"You're fun to look at." I shrugged, fighting my own smile. He leaned forward, pursing his lips in a silent request for a kiss. I obliged, feeling the familiar tingle that started from my toes and traveled all the way to my head, whenever we kissed. I'd been scared that feeling would go away, but somehow, even after two full years of being together it hadn't.

"This doesn't distract from the fact that I was right. You were not prepared to make dinner." He replied, as soon as our lips disconnected. "I'd like to hear you say it."

"No."

"Audrey Bennett, I promise if you don't say it, I'll make you regret it." He grinned, glancing down at my lips before slowly bringing his eyes back up to mine. I felt a tingle of anticipation in the pit of my stomach. His gaze traveled down to my lips again and then my chest, lingering on my breasts. I could feel my nipples harden as he licked his lips slowly. "How much time do we have before they get here?" His voice was husky, full of desire and longing. I clenched my legs together, surprised but incredibly turned on at the sudden shift of mood.

The ring of the doorbell was like a splash of cold water, immediately dampening the mood. Montrell groaned and shifted his stance. "Saved by the bell," he mumbled.

"I'll go grab the door." I grinned and gently squeezed his erection. He hissed a breath through his teeth, briefly closing his eyes so he could steady himself. He gently pressed himself against my hand, leaning into my touch.

"Don't do that unless you want me to ruin this entire dinner."

"Control yourself." I giggled, heading to the front door. Deja, Monae, and Brina all stood on my front porch, holding various food items. I hadn't asked them to bring anything, but I'd had a feeling Montrell had been conspiring against me while I was struggling to find something to make. I stepped aside so they could come in and pointed to the kitchen. "Hey girls, go ahead and put your items in the kitchen. We're almost ready." Chili circled around their legs in an excited greeting, making Deja almost trip over her stocky and fluffy frame.

"Watch out, Chili!" Deja huffed, lightly pushing her out of the way. "If I mess around and step on your tail, you're going to think I did you wrong."

"Where's the turkey?" Monae asked. I stifled a laugh at the withering look Montrell gave me and shrugged.

"It's right here!" Mekhi called as he and Elodie came walking in, fifteen-year-old Kellan lumbering in behind them, carrying a tray with a turkey shaped lump covered in aluminum foil. A bright, obviously relieved smile spread across Montrell's face. I wanted to throw the hand towel draped across my shoulder at him. I should have known he would have discreetly called his brother to bail him out when he realized that I wasn't prepared to make the dinner. I couldn't even be mad though; I appreciated our people coming together to make sure we had a dinner that was memorable. I could always count on my girls to help me out, and now that Mekhi had become a part of the family, I was learning that I could count on him too.

"My brother, my brother! You always come through!" He exclaimed. I rolled my eyes and closed the door behind them. Kellan placed the turkey on the counter and looked around.

"Where's your Christmas tree?" He asked, there was a hint of disappointment in his voice.

"It's only Thanksgiving!" I replied, shaking my head, he was just as bad as Elodie when it came to Christmas spirit. If they had any say, the Christmas tree would be up on Halloween.

"Come on, Auntie!" He sighed. "You have to do better than that. The tree goes up on November first. You know this."

"Maybe in your house!" I stuck my tongue out at him. "But not in mine. At least wait until Black Friday." I would not be bullied into putting my tree up early, no matter how cute his dimples were. I wouldn't be swayed. He laughed at me before turning his attention to Chili who was waiting patiently for him to acknowledge her. I had no idea my dog was such a sucker for male attention. Whenever Kellan or Montrell were around, she paid me dust.

"Okay, so now that we are all here, Elodie and I have some news." Mekhi called out.

"You two going on the road together?" Monae asked, clasping her hands together dreamily. "That would be so romantic."

"No, not quite. Haven't been on the road in a while." Montrell replied with a soft laugh. He wrapped his arm around Elodie's shoulders with a gentle squeeze. She grinned up at him, unable to contain her excitement.

"It's been so hard trying to keep it a secret." Elodie beamed and held up her hand. On her ring finger, a red ruby round cut engagement ring sparkled in the light. It was different, but it was incredibly Elodie. The color was similar to the red dress she wore during their first Christmas musical together, right around the time they had officially started dating. A chorus of ear-piercing screams filled the room as all four of us raced towards our friend. I reached her first and snatched her hand so I could get a good look at the ring.

"Oh my God! El!" I gasped. Tears pricking my eyes. Montrell clapped his brother on the back with a smile.

"You did a good job, bro!" He exclaimed.

"All because of a journal." I smiled, with a shake of my head. Deja and Brina both rolled their eyes.

"You and that journal!" Brina laughed. "I can't believe Elodie managed to trick you into believing that thing is real."

"It's not a trick." Elodie and I both said at the same time. Everyone turned to look at us.

"Matter of fact," I began, "Let me go grab it. I'll be right back." I ran to my room to grab the journal that had sat untouched on my bookshelf for the last two years. I had been expecting it to shift immediately, as soon as Montrell and I had agreed to give this relationship a shot, but it didn't.

But now, as I carried the journal back out to my friends, it felt a little lighter than usual. I had periodically taken it down to reread through our story whenever I got bored and the pages had felt different. I placed the journal on the counter in front of everyone and motioned for Brina to open it.

"You've never actually taken a look at it."

"I don't need to read it, I was there. I saw what happened," she shrugged. Elodie shot me a look over her shoulder. Mekhi and Montrell, who were both familiar with the journal and its abilities, exchanged a look as well.

"Open it." I replied. Brina sighed and pulled the journal towards her. When she opened it, I half expected her to skim over the words, but to my complete surprise, it was entirely empty. She thumbed through some of the pages and then turned to me, confused.

"How am I supposed to read it if there's nothing in it? Did you erase it or something?"

"What?" I grabbed the journal and flipped through it myself in disbelief. I hadn't erased anything out of it. The words had been written in pen. It was impossible for it to have been erased, yet the journal was blank. Each page looked like it had never been touched. Every word of our story, completely gone.

"Here we go." Mekhi whispered, grabbing Elodie's hand. She smiled knowingly up at him.

Kellan peered over my shoulder, wide-eyed. "Whoa, it still works."

"What's happening?" I looked up at Elodie, confused.

"It's working." She whispered. The journal began to vibrate in my hands. I put it back on the counter and stepped back. A nervous hush fell over the room as we all watched it rumble and shake against the table. The cover flew open, and the pages began to flip aggressively, making a loud whoosh sound as they turned.

We all stood there in awe, too scared to get close, but too interested to look away. The journal kept moving as if something we couldn't see was turning the pages for us. It kept moving until it reached the last page and then fell still. Words, in a different script than what I was used to seeing appeared on the page. I nudged Brina who shot a terrified glance at me.

"I'm not touching that thing!" She exclaimed, trying to slide away. Elodie sighed and stepped forward to grab it.

"It's not going to hurt you, girl. It's just going to tell you who needs the journal next."

"You say that as if it's a totally normal occurrence to have a journal write in itself in weird ink." Brina snapped. Elodie slid the journal closer to get a good look at what it said and then pushed it towards Brina.

"Well, you'll have to get used to it. Because it's your turn."

We all inched forward to see what the journal said. I was sad that my story was completely gone, but excited to see what it meant for my girl Brina. If it brought her someone that could match her step for step, then I absolutely wanted to see that happen for her. I wanted to see that happen to all of my girls.

"What do you mean 'my turn'? How are you not freaking out right now?" She grabbed the journal and looked down at it, brows knitting in an expression of confusion mixed with fear. Six words stared back at her in loopy script.

THiS JOURNAL BELONGS TO BRiNA JONES

About The Author

Lauren Roach is a dog obsessed, true-crime loving, self-proclaimed book nerd that has always dreamed of becoming a published author. While most kids were frolicking in the sun, Lauren chose the path less sweaty and opted for the cool embrace of air conditioning while immersed in a book or busily penning fan fictions about whatever heartthrob boy band was on her radar.

Lauren's literary ambitions took a brief hiatus when she decided to venture into the world of criminal justice, earning both a bachelor's and a master's degree in the field. Even though she has yet to use either one of her degrees for anything career-related, she hopes to maybe use her criminal justice knowledge to one day write a really good mystery plot.

Fast forward to today, Lauren is happily residing in North Carolina with her lovely husband where she starts celebrating Christmas in August and isn't afraid to break out a book in the middle of a social gathering. You can follow her work at

Instagram & Threads: @thebookybabe_
Tik Tok & Bluesky: @thebookybabe
Twitter (X): @LaurenRWrites
Podcast: Lauren's Library Podcast
Website: www.sunflowerrosepublishing.com